ELEPHANT BANGS TRAIN

WILLIAM KOTZWINKLE

NEW YORK

PANTHEON BOOKS

A DIVISION OF RANDOM HOUSE

ELEPHANT
BANGS
TRAIN

For Elizabeth

With thanks to Bob Shiarella

CONTENTS

"Somewhere there was once a Flower, a Stone,
a Crystal, a Queen, a King, a Palace, a Lover and his
Beloved, and this was long ago, on an Island somewhere
in the ocean five thousand years ago . . . Such is Love,
the Mystic Flower of the soul. This is the Centre,
the Self . . ."

Jung to Miguel Serrano
A Record of Two Friendships

ELEPHANT BANGS TRAIN

A
Most
Incredible
Meal

In 1843, a Siberian woodcutter, Alexei Bulnovka, while walking homeward in the moonlight, noticed a deep shadow in a mountain of ice. The wind howled, stinging and freezing his face. He'd been thinking of a fire, food and his bed, but dropping to his hands and knees, he crawled along the frozen hillside, trying to determine the nature and size of the dark shape within it.

The moon was nearly full. The woodcutter swung his axe. Three strokes were enough to crack the ice. Bulnovka knelt and reached into the opening with his bare hand. His fingers touched coarse stiff hair. He scraped away the clinging ice until he uncovered beneath the hair, a toe, large as a fist, hard as stone.

He looked around the frozen hill, caught in a cold wave of fear that iced his spirit. Yet as in that terrible moment when a great tree is falling, he felt a surging joy.

He began to chop. The ice broke, slid away. He uncovered a foot, enormous, with the stone toenails of a giant. Whose foot, he dared not imagine. He knew only that he had to free the creature from its icy grave.

He struck with his axe, again and again, and soon his body was drenched with sweat. He was a powerful man, his blows were shattering; yet his limbs were like twigs compared to the hairy leg which was slowly revealed beneath his strokes, a leg like the trunk of a hundred-year oak. With woodcutter's precision, he aimed his axe so that it fragmented the ice, but did not wound the flesh frozen beneath.

The night passed on, but he'd lost track of time. He'd been a steady fellow, quiet and unfulfilled. Now he was intoxicated with discovery, and all that he had ever been, boy, young man, husband and father, seemed to culminate in this task of liberation.

He did not tire as he worked, but like the sculptor, quickly learned the technique of making those blows which fracture deep cavities in stone, and huge slides of ice fell away with echoing cracks.

He cut steps and mounted upward on the ice, chopping through to the creature's haunches, which were big as oxen. His joy was great, he made songs.

What were the courts of the Czar compared to this, the hidden treasure? He strode across the glistening ledge of ice, striking boldly. What were troops, and horses, compared to this, the gigantus?

A massive chunk of ice fell away and there, staring coldly at him, was an eye, shining in the moonlight like a jewel. Removing his glove, he touched the small frozen pupil. Like all men, he'd nourished the idea of a miracle, but now he knew, his companion was dead. The eye was open; the expression, a mournful one, was still there, but the great spirit had fled. Alexei Bulnovka was alone.

He continued chopping, and slowly the top of the head appeared, a terrific mass of bone and flesh, covered by a shaggy mane. He stood upon it in the falling snow, facing the eastern sky, and knew his first moment of doubt. Might it not be better to let the snow reclaim its prisoner? The beast, whatever it was, was dead, preserved like a precious saint. Who was he to disturb its sleep?

He staggered down the icy staircase he'd constructed, and looked into the beady frozen eye. He longed to see the face of this creature. Decisively, he struck a blow between and just below the eyes, parting the ice around a long protuberance, like a giant's arm.

He looked up at the sky, questioning the stars. He struck again. The side of his axe collided with something hard, like bone. Knocking away the ice, he saw that it was not a bone, but a long curling tooth, like the Saracen sword, and then he knew he'd found the grandfather of elephants and he chopped with fury through the night.

As the grey morning came, Alexei Bulnovka's axe had revealed the head, forequarters, and midsection of the beast. The mastodon stood erect, except for the right front leg,

5   A MOST INCREDIBLE MEAL

which was bent, as if in kneeling. Bulnovka knelt beside it, resting his feverish head against the frozen flesh.

A dream he had as a child erupted in his mind—he'd been walking across a frozen lake and seen below, frozen in the ice, a diamond. Here was that diamond, he realized, risen from the waters of time, and he wept, knowing that this night had been, after all, the one moment of his life.

The work Alexei Bulnovka had performed alone in the night became public property with the dawn. As when the grave of the Redeemer was opened and the flame of his rising body touched every heart, so the lifting of the icy shroud was seen in a dream by the oldest woman of nearby Solmuchkava, as the sleepy village awakened restlessly to its most glorious dawn.

Barking dogs led the way to the mastodon and the men of the village followed with their axes, along with the women and old Petroyuv the priest, who sprinkled holy water on the beast and gave Alexei Bulnovka the sacred host in the snow. In a few hours the carcass was fully loosed from its glacial sarcophagus and was claimed by Count Ivan Fyodorvich Musov, whose team of superb black horses was dwarfed in the shadow of the mastodon.

Count Musov was, momentarily, speechless, and walked quietly around the great beast, slapping lightly once with his whip the kneeling leg.

News of Count Musov's find was quickly carried to the city of Svobodny, where, within the following hour, a train for Solmuchkava was boarded by Rushov, a physician of the Czar, and Nyam Gogoli, a wandering poet who convinced the conductor that in the interest of Russian literature he should be allowed to ride for free to the site of the primeval grave.

Doctor and poet arrived at the grave site by late afternoon, when makeshift tents and cookstoves were dotting the ice, and the men of the village were in counsel with Count Musov about the removal of the body.

Seeing the beast, Gogoli the poet was seized by vertigo, as if he'd been hurled from a mountain of the moon. Rushov the physician declared the mastodon to be a female and suggested to Count Musov that it be removed to Moscow. But how could it be moved? There was no railroad car big enough to handle her, and now that her snowsuit had been removed, she would soon begin to melt.

However, the mastodon was still frozen solid and stood unwavering in the snow, eyes staring out over the once-silent tundra, which was now filled with spectators.

The logistics of movement were grappled with by Count Musov and the village men. The hero of the night, Alexei Bulnovka, could not be consulted, as he lay inside a tent, covered in blankets brought by the women, who watched over his deep and dreamless sleep.

There was no team of horses strong enough to draw the mastodon over the fifteen miles to Count Musov's castle, not if every horse in Solmuchkava were harnessed to her carcass. The only way of moving her was in pieces. So the question was, which piece?

Ultimately, the head was decided upon, because of the fine-tooled ivory which Count Musov envisioned in his main gallery. The physician of the Czar instructed the men as to where the easiest cutting would be, and as night fell the woodsmen took their axes to the great neck and in the flickering firelight began to chop away, to no avail. The flesh was harder than Russian oak.

Saws were brought and manned by teams in the moonlight, but progress was pitiably slow. Finally, it was decided amongst the men that they should wait until the thawing of the beast had begun. The workmen retired to the village for the night; Count Musov and the Czar's physician rode off to the castle. Still sleeping, Alexei Bulnovka was carried home on a sled, pulled by Gogoli the poet. The woodcutter was attended through the night by his wife and daughter, who sat up over a glowing samovar; the poet dropped off to sleep in a chair, into dreams of a tropical rain forest, where stampeded the pachyderms of paradise.

Dawn came once again on the ancient hulk, bathing her in sunlight. The village teams returned, as did the Count, and his wife, the beautiful Katerina Dupinovna, who'd been given a thorough examination that morning, following her bath, by the physician of the Czar, who declared her pulse to be normal, in spite of the excitement.

The woodcutter and the poet had been first to arrive, and now stood watching the industry of the men. The work was proceeding satisfactorily, as drops of blood could be seen on the neck of the mastodon where the saber-toothed saws were cutting through the hide, now softer and more yielding.

"I was a fool," said Bulnovka, cursing himself.

"You held her in the moonlight," said the poet.

At noon the spinal column was cracked, and the tendons of the neck severed. The ice was bathed in blood, and the great head dropped off. The ivory tusks rested in the snow like the runners of a sleigh. A horse was hitched to each one and over the ice field the head rode, eyes open, toward the castle of Count Musov.

"Might I suggest," said the physician, indicating the flank of the beast, "that you now carve steaks?"

The men of the village worked skillfully, cutting off great hunks of flesh, which were then salted, wrapped, and taken immediately to the castle. The Count was not ungenerous. Each man received a cut of meat larger than his own torso, as did Father Petroyuv for himself and his housekeeper.

In the afternoon, under the mournful gaze of Alexei Bulnovka, the kneeling leg collapsed and the mastodon tumbled over, as the workmen leapt from their posts, and bloody axes flew in the air.

"A banquet tonight!" shouted Count Musov, waving to the woodcutter and the poet. The poet nodded his head. The woodcutter stared out over the frozen field.

The feet of the beast were chopped off and loaded into Count Musov's sleigh, as the sun set behind the icy mountain range. The remaining fragments were left in the snow, unattended, except for small birds who searched the hair for ancient fleas.

Bulnovka and the poet walked toward the village.

"I'll not sit at his table," said the woodcutter.

"My dear fellow," said the poet, "you must see the final curtain."

The poet prevailed and that night a horse and sleigh were borrowed from the blacksmith. The two men set out for the castle, riding in silence across the glistening fields, past the dimly lit church where Father Petroyuv knelt alone.

Upon the altar, between two candles, was a piece of bone from the kneeling leg of the mammoth. "O Ghost," prayed the old priest, "forgive us." He ran his fingers along the bone, then removing his high stiff hat, leaned his grey head over and laid a kiss upon the cold smooth surface.

Fires burned in the Count's courtyard, and the air was filled with the shouts of men and the music of stringed instruments. Bulnovka and the poet were led into the main gallery to a huge table surrounded by guests and filled with jugs of vodka. The Count and his beloved Katerina Dupinovna sat at the head, and Musov raised his glass to greet the latest arrivals to his table.

"The hero of Solmuchkava!" toasted the Count, and those at the table cheered drunkenly as Bulnovka and the poet took their seats. Spirits were high; the transparent drink of fire had stoked every heart. "Come, Bulnovka," said the poet, clicking his glass against that of the woodcutter, who drained his cup with a sudden and startling ferociousness.

Count Musov stood, waved his hand in the air. Katerina Dupinovna clapped her small white hands. Silence fell in the room. "We have a treat in store for us," said the Count, eyes glazed with glory. "I have opened the oldest wine. It is only fitting." The Count's servants entered with a large cask. "I am told," he smiled, "that in China they eat thousand-year-old eggs. Tonight Count Musov's guests shall dine on a beast—how old do you estimate it to be, Doctor?"

The doctor rose precariously, supporting himself with one

hand on the back of his chair. "At least two thousand years," he said drunkenly, and slid back down.

"At least two thousand years," said the Count in a solemn echo, and gestured to his kitchen. The servants entered once again, bearing an enormous piece of meat on a silver platter, which they set in the middle of the long wooden table. "I shall carve," said the Count, and the plates of the guests, noble men and women from as far as Krasnoyar, were filled, each with a large red-running piece of the mammoth.

The Count, still standing, bowed his head.

"We thank Thee for this bountiful table," he said, and stabbing a piece of meat on the end of his knife, held it in the air for a moment, then dropped it in his mouth.

The table burst into applause and the doctor rose in his seat. "More ice!" he shouted, waving his glass. He fell back in his chair, laughing to himself. He'd watched the cook's men beating the meat with mallets.

The poet disliked the flesh of any beast or fish, but tonight he was gripped by a dark hunger. He laid a piece of the ancient meat on his tongue, and chewed into it.

The woodcutter stared at his plate, unable to recall the song he'd sung in the moonlight.

"A most incredible meal," said the Count, slicing through the roast with his ivory-handled knife.

"Superb, my darling," said his wife, nibbling with little white teeth. Upstairs, the maids were braiding her a wig of hair from the mammoth.

"We have indeed been blessed," said the doctor, laying his hand in the lap of the young woman beside him, who seemed not to notice it had landed there, so professional were the good doctor's learned fingers. "More ice, my dear?" he asked, dropping a glistening chunk into the young lady's glass, followed by more of the clear, inflaming potion. Vodka, thought the doctor, his brain reeling, is a supernatural drink.

The poet's eyes were closed. His arms were pressed back in his chair and he had surrendered. The primeval meat was in him now, and his soul was dancing.

Count Musov chewed heroically on the rubbery flesh. What a beast! And herds of them once, with their ivory bayonets. A sudden surge of power raced through his body, thrilling him, and then suddenly, his head felt heavy, as if it were made of stone.

"You look as if you'd swallowed the thousand-year-old egg, my dear," said his wife with a smile, sucking the meaty juices off her fingers.

The three musicians plucked out the mood from their corner of the hall. They'd eaten and drunk and now they pursued the mammoth's ghost, constructing chords they'd never known before, weaving dark songs to capture her.

Alexei Bulnovka pushed back his plate, stood, and walking to the head of the table, contemplated driving the ivory-handled knife of Count Musov into his own heart, then considered driving it into Count Musov.

"Well, woodcutter, what is it?" joked the Count. "Is there some trophy you would like, the tail, perhaps?"

Bulnovka turned and walked out of the hall, as the beautiful Katerina Dupinovna burst into laughter.

"These men of the fields," Count Musov explained to his guests, "they're made of ice."

The poet sank in his chair, down past broken temples,

and the scattered pots of civilization, down past the tribes of men, and down, until all trace of humanity was eclipsed and there was only the trumpeting of beasts, and all belonged to them, and still he hurtled down, through the gates of dawn.

"Delicious, delicious," said the doctor, laying his head on his plate and closing his eyes to rest in the primal gravy.

The woodcutter walked in the snow, breathing in the cold crystal of the night. His steps carried him to the rear of the castle, to a room lit by the glow of several lamps, in which the head of the mastodon sat, like an icon.

He entered the room, wherein was working a taxidermist from Poplova who'd arrived that afternoon. The massive head rested on a table, tusks curling in the lamplight, and the old man was painting the skin of its head with translucent fluid. He saluted Bulnovka, and lifting the lip of the mastodon, pointed inside.

"Buttercups," he said, and extracted a small yellow flower from the great row of teeth.

Marie

MARIE COBBINSKI picked up her dress. We could see her legs, Ducky Doodle, Ralph Jenkins, and me. A summer wind blew through the room. Paper birds flapped on the window. Life was sweet, we were young, teacher was in the hall.

"Ya, ya!" yelled Ducky Doodle. "Last day in second grade!"

The meadow tossed its perfume. A serpent danced in the sunlit grass. The earth was turning.

"I wore my tap shoes today," said Marie. Intoxicated, we stared at her knees.

"Higher, please," said Ralph Jenkins.

Marie rose from her seat and stood before us in the aisle, blond, beautiful, if a bit too full in the nose. She smiled shyly, tugged her dress up higher. Openmouthed, we stared. The class was sailing airplanes. We were hidden in delight, beside the papier-mâché mountain in the corner.

"Show us your panties, Marie," suggested Ralph Jenkins. Ducky Doodle drummed on his head. I said, "Oh, Marie."

Swept up in our admiration, she twirled in the sunlight, as a flower opened inside her, and the wind dove in the window, beguiling her. Unable to resist, she showed her panties.

Our souls reeled. The distant ages wheeled into view. Ducky the Jester stood on his hands. Ralph Jenkins wiggled his ears. Our princess skipped down the aisle, holding up her dress with two fingers. The lilac bush beat on the windowpane. How nice her black two-shoes tapped.

"More panties!" yelled Ralph, wet-mouthed, calling the toast.

Over the seven hills of the valley came the summer goddess, trailing her veils. Marie bent over, threw her dress up from behind.

Her panties were as white as Christ's linen, pure as the summer, filled with promises, sweet, untouched by vacationing boys. We buzzed around her, drawn by her delicate essence, her petalling prepubescence. She danced, we sang, teacher was forever down the hall, splashing in the fountain.

The clock ticked and jumped. We had the answer. It was Marie Cobbinski, Ducky Doodle, Ralph Jenkins, and me. We cut the moorings, sailed away, out of the classroom and into the air. There, in the sky, the trapeze: I am swung from it, she catches me, we hang, suspended. I gaze into the face of love, uncertain if I am Ralph, or Ducky, or me, when suddenly, we are upended. The high wire is broken, the team is falling.

"What is going on in this room?"

Marie's eyes crossed, she bit her lip.

Standing in the doorway was the teacher, a musty old bird of gloom, eggs petrified inside her. Cackling, she ran to her perch in front of the room.

Ducky and I wheeled in front of Marie. She pulled down her dress. Teacher didn't see the panties, she was scratching in her nest. "Marie Cobbinski, get to your seat immediately!" she said, and charged down the aisle with a ruler.

Marie ran to her seat. We stood frozen beneath the beak of the hoarfrost bird. "How dare you!" she shrieked, snapping Ducky Doodle by the suspenders. "Hey, hey," was all he could say. "How dare you interrupt this class with your—" She smacked Doodle on the head. "—antics! Now *sit*," she said, and catapulted him down the aisle.

She turned to me. There were the little people in the village under the mountain, working with their rakes and shovels. "Who do you think *you* are?" she asked.

"Nobody," I said.

"That's right," she said. "Hold out your hands!"

The ruler came down. There was a fire in my palms. I looked up. Taking my head in her claw, she clamped me in my seat.

Ralph Jenkins stood alone, wet-mouthed and surprised. The class laughed. Ralph was a dumbbell. He'd catch hell.

Head trembling, she went for him, past the open window.

The wind caught her hair, waved it aloft. "Oh," she said, touching her bald spot. "Why do you torment me?"

She sailed toward Ralph, a Chinese dragon kite, red-faced and terrible, flapping her horny tail. "I'll teach you," she said. Ralph ran to the window, tried to fly, it was too late. He searched the sky, hoping to jump the room, but the summer goddess was playing with other boys in the valley, boys on the loose and miles away. The magic was ended. The dragon kite descended like a goblin from the moon.

Beating her bony wings, she nested on him, pressing his head into her ribs, burying him in her paper gown. He was doomed, he was going under. He tried to save himself. He yelled the secret.

"Marie Cobbinski showed her panties!"

The earth stopped, the wind died, the dragon kite collapsed into an old woman. Far away in the next county, the summer goddess shuddered, fell to the grass.

"Yeah, yeah!" screamed Ralph Jenkins, unable to bear the silence he'd created with the enormity of his curse.

I looked at Marie. Her head was down. She was crying. The class was laughing. They would sing, *we saw your panties.*

"Marie, I'm ashamed of you," said the teacher. She walked slowly to the front of the room, climbed wearily onto her perch. So this is how it ends, she thought. This is how they leave me.

17   MARIE

Follow
The
Eagle

JOHNNY EAGLE climbed onto his 750-cubic-centimeter Arupa motorcycle and roared out of the Navaho Indian Reservation, followed by the Mexican, Domingo, on a rattling Japanese cycle stolen from a Colorado U law student.

Up the morning highway they rode toward the Colorado River, half-drunk and full-crazy in the sunlight, Eagle's slouch hat brim bent in the wind, Domingo's long black moustaches trailing in the air.

Yes, thought Eagle, wheeling easy over the flat land, yes indeed. And they came to Navaho Canyon where they shut down their bikes. Mist from the winding river far below rose up through the scarred plateau and the air was still.

Eagle and Domingo wheeled their bikes slowly to the edge of the Canyon. Domingo got off and threw a stone across the gorge. It struck the far wall, bounced, echoed, fell away in silence.

"Long way to the other side, man," he said, looking at Eagle.

Eagle said nothing, sat on his bike, staring across the gaping crack in the earth.

Domingo threw another stone, which cleared the gap, kicking up a little cloud of dust on top of the other cliff. "How fast you got to go—hunnert, hunnert twenty-five?"

Eagle spit into the canyon and tromped the starter of his bike.

"When you goin', man?" shouted Domingo over the roar.

"Tomorrow!"

That night was a party for Johnny Eagle on the Reservation. He danced with Red Wing in the long house, pressed her up against a corner. Medicine Man came by, gave Eagle a cougar tooth. "I been talkin' to it, Eagle," he said.

"Thanks, man," said Eagle and he put it around his neck and took Red Wing back to his shack, held her on the falling porch in the moonlight, looked at the moon over her shoulder.

She lay on his broken bed, hair undone on his ragged pillow, her buckskin jacket on the floor. Through the open window came music from the party, guitar strings and a drum head and Domingo singing

"Don't go tomorrow," said Red Wing, unbuttoning Eagle's cowboy shirt.

"Gitchimanito is watchin' out for me, baby," said Eagle, and he mounted her, riding bareback, up the draw, slow, to the drumbeat. His eyes were closed but he saw her tears, like silver beads, and he rode faster and shot his arrow through the moon.

"Oh, Johnny," she moaned, quivering beneath him, "don't go," and he felt her falling away, down the waving darkness.

They lay, looking out through the window. He hung the cat's tooth around her neck. "Stay with me," she said, holding him till dawn, and he rose up while she was sleeping. The Reservation was grey, the shacks crouching in the dawn light.

Eagle shook Domingo out of his filthy bed. The Mexican crawled across the floor, looking for his sombrero, and they walked across the camp to the garage where the pickup truck was stowed with Eagle's bike.

Eagle pulled the cycle off the kickstand and they rolled it up a wooden ramp into the back of the truck, then slid the ramp in the truck, roped it down, and drove quietly off the Reservation.

They went down the empty highway, Domingo at the wheel, Eagle slouched in the corner by the door. "Why you doin' this, man?" asked the Mexican, not looking at Eagle.

Eagle's hat was over his eyes. He slept a little, nodding with the bounces in and out of a dream. His head dropped against the cold window. The truck was stopped.

Eagle stepped down onto the silent mesa. My legs shakin', he thought and went round to the back of the truck, where Domingo was letting down the ramp. Eagle touched the cold handlebars of the bike and stopped shaking. They wheeled the cycle to the ground.

"I know a chick," said Domingo. They pushed the ramp to the edge of the canyon. "—with a fantastic ass—" They faced the ramp to the misty hole, bracing it with cinder blocks. "She live down in Ensenada, man, whattya say we go down there?"

Eagle climbed onto the bike, turned over the motor, breaking the morning stillness. He circled slowly, making bigger circles until the motor was running strong, then drove over to Domingo at the edge of the ramp.

"Buena suerte, amigo!" shouted the Mexican over the roaring engine.

"On the other side!" called Eagle, and drove away from the ramp, fifty, a hundred, two, three, four hundred yards. He turned, lined the bike up with the ramp. A white chicken fluttered in his stomach. Domingo waved his black hat.

In neutral, Eagle gunned the big Arupa engine, once, twice, and engaging first gear spun out toward the ramp.

The sun was rising, the speedometer climbing as he shifted into second gear, fifty, sixty, seventy, eighty miles an hour. Eagle burned across the table land toward Navaho Canyon, into third gear, ninety, a hundred, had jumped twelve cars on this bike, had no job, saw Domingo from the corner of his eye, was going one twenty-five and that was it as he hit the ramp and sailed his ass off into space.

The cycle whined above the mist, floating like a thunder

clap, and Johnny Eagle in his slouch hat rode lightly as an arrow, airborne in the glory of the moment as a sunbeam struck him in his arc of triumph, then his sunset came upon him and he saw the flaw in his life story, *one fifty, man, not one twenty-five,* as the far cliff for which he hungered came no closer, seemed to mock him through the mist, was impossible, always had been, and his slouch hat blew away.

Don't go, Johnny.

He strained to lift his falling horse, to carry her above the morning, to fly with her between his legs, rupturing several muscles in his passion and then as he fell for certain just clung sadly with the morning rising up his asshole, poor balls groaning Johnny Eagle, falling down Navaho Canyon, the geological formations quite apparent as the mist was clearing from the rock.

"SO LONG, MAN!" he shouted, with quite a way to go, falling like a regular comet, smoke and fire out the tailpipe as the bike turned slowly over, plunging through the hollow entry. Jesus Christ my blood is boiling there goes the engine.

He fell quietly, hissing through the mist, dreaming it was still dawn on Red Wing's red-brown thighs.

Johnny, don't go. O.K. babe I'll stay here.

But he saw the real rocks rushing past him.

I uster dance. Neck down in the fender. She held me in my screwloose, Johnny Eagle, be my old man, babe I'm crazy and mus' go to Gitchegumee.

Down in Ensenada man

Domingo falling to the barroom laughing with his knife blade bloody, my look at that terra cotter there like faces in the Canyon, Sheriff you kin let us out now, won't do no harm. There goes my shoes man where am I.

A fantastic

Water like rock. Thousand fist pound my brain out. Crack me, shell me, awful snot death crap death hunnert bucks that bike death cost me black death o no Colorado do not take me.

Yes I took you Johnny Eagle

Wham the arrow crossed the morning. I am shot from out my body whooooooooooooooo the endless sunrise.

Some time later a fledgling eagle was hatched by an old white-headed fierce-beaked queen of the Canyon. She pushed the little eagle into space where he learned to soar, crying *kyreeeee,* high above the morning, turning in the mist upon the wind.

And Domingo, riding down to Ensenada, to see the girl in Ensenada, crossed the border singing

> *He saw Aunt Mary comin' an'*
> *He duck back in the alley*

The Doorman

CHARLES SAT by the window, watching. Outside the buildings made faces. Look Charles we are old and cracked. On the street below the stone people moved slowly and Charles watched them six thousand years.

"Lift your feet," said Mother, riding on her rag stick.

"I'm talking to the buildings," said Charles.

"No, you're not, dear, lift your feet so Mother can clean."

Charles lifted his feet like a good person. Mother waved her rag stick at the dirties who lived on the floor and they flew up in the sunlight. One was named Susan and one Betty Ann and Carol too, dirty girls make sissy and cucky.

"Help me with your father," said Mother. Charles stood

up, turned around six times and walked to the chair in the living room, where Father was snoring birds out his nose.

"Lift his feet up."

Charles lifted up the feet, and Mother made the dirties fly.

"I am the stove," said Charles.

"No, you're not, dear, put Daddy's feet down."

"Yes, I am a greasy stove."

"Charles, I cleaned that stove this morning with Ajax," said wipe-me-mommy. "Did you find dirt on it somewhere?"

"Dirty! Cucky and sissy!" Charles ran into the bathroom and slammed the door six times.

"What's going on?" shouted Father. "I'm trying to rest my eyes!"

"Charles, do you have to sissy?"

"Sissy!" shouted Father. "He's thirty-five years old!"

"He's sick."

"I'm sick, too. Of your sissy."

"Charles, what are you doing in the bathroom? Do you want me to help you?"

The door opened and he was not alone.

"Is it number one or number two, Charles?"

"One o'clock two o'clock."

"Come along, dear, you don't have to do anything." His hand stuck in her arm, the fly was caught. Mister Horrible walked alongside whispering Why don't you kill her, Charles?

"Help!" cried Charles. Yes, bash her head in kill her. No said Good Nobody, bite Mister Thumb, bite bite bite

"Charles, you'll bite your thumb off!"

I am a meat market.

"Are you all right?"

"I'm dead."

"No, you're not, dear."

"You know," said Father, "this place is a zoo."

"It's time you were awake, Anthony, you've got things to do."

Charles is buried in a dark place uptown. The lights are out except one candle. There are no airplanes, not even the mayor.

"I don't have to do anything," said Father. "I work all week to pay the rent on this looney bin."

"Why don't we all have a nice cup of tea?" said Mother, and cups came out of her hand.

Charles sat down three times. This cup, hello, is cracked, and so the movie came on. The cowboy shot in the air. The girls behind Charles giggled. Charles is cracked, they said. He crawled away under the seats through the popcorn.

"Charles, get off the floor." Father's upside-down face came looking.

"Cracky popcorn." How did I get under the table.

"Sit up, Charles, it's our favorite English breakfast tea."

Yes, sit up, Charles, that's a good lunatic. Look at the faces in the ceiling.

"I read in the barbershop," said Father blowing in his tea, "popcorn is first in pernicious effect on the human body."

"You spend too much time at that barbershop."

"I suppose I should cut my own hair."

"Have a biscuit, Charles."

"Gobble, gobble." Stuff it, up your nose, in your ear.

"Eat your biscuit nicely, darling, you're not a savage."

Get out of the kitchen, Charles, she's trying to poison our monkey. Stand up, push back chair.

"What do you say, dear?"

"Ankle bush."

"You say excuse me."

"Yes sir." Into the living room with Mister pig snake rooster, what do you say, excuse me. The chair is breathing. Executives like yourself use our credit card anywhere.

Into the bedroom the quiet Mommy room. Oogly boogly nighttime squeak noises come from under here. Squeak squeak oh squeak squeak Anthony squeak squeak I love squeak you squeak

"Charles, come out from under there! Anthony, Charles is under the bed."

"Maybe he's tired. I'm tired."

"Charles, you'll get all dusty, though God knows I cleaned under there this morning."

I am a chair.

"Go on, Charles, get out. Mother has to dress."

Marching marching one two three to living Vietnam room marching round and round

"Relax, will you, Charles, and let your old man pull himself together." The old man and the couch were stuck together. Charles rode on a ball which grew larger, then smaller, then crushed him.

Thump thump thump thump

"What the hell goes on in this house!" Father devils came out with little forks, blue and red, let's have a birthday party Charles is five.

27 THE DOORMAN

Thump through the wallpaper thump down the lane thump you are magic thump here comes Mother.

"Charles, stop banging your head against the wall."

"I work like a dog all week," said Father, "and on my day off, him."

"Charles, how would you like to go the store for Mother?"

Thump over the rim thump miles away thump gone

"Come into the kitchen, dear," said Mother, sticking Charles to her arm, "and we'll make a list."

Mommy wrecked the nice trip, said Mister Ugly, and is a spider.

You be quiet, Charles is going to the store as if he was somebody. I'll wear the tablecloth and you throw her out the window.

"Come here, dear, Mother will pin the note on."

"Nacky nacka."

"Hold still, Charles."

"Cracky cracka."

"When you go in the store, show the man the note."

"Mickey Mouse."

"Charles, are you feeling all right?"

"Mister Postcard, hello."

"Are you too sick to go today?"

Be quiet or she won't let you out. Punch yourself in the arm ten times, it'll help.

"Stop punching yourself, Charles, you'll get cancer. Here's a dollar, now put it in your pocket."

Charles walked toward the faraway door with his stone feet five thousand years

"Don't get lost and don't be long."

Just go through the door and don't say anything looney or she'll follow you like she used to follow you to school.

"Be careful, Charles."

Charles tried to control his legs so they wouldn't walk sideways down the wall. One two these are steps. The walls are certainly old, look at that moss.

Paul Fishey hit him in the head with a stone. Sonofabitch. The hallway is empty. We'll see you Easter, Gladys.

You been put on earth for a special mission, don't get lost. On your own planet you are a big shot, over.

Just whistling like a person. Don't jump out the bright window. Don't bump anybody.

Just a flight of steps. Sister, I'm stuck to my desk I can't get loose. Now Charles you must stop disrupting this class. Step just steps down we go and there's the bottom, see? Life's not so bad.

A door opened marked 2. Charles waved his foot. The fat lady came out in her fat lady. Six thousand years I'm stepping toward you

"Hello, Charles."

"Hello, Mrs. Whatsyourname." Clicking his fingers behind his back not to get bitten, he walked down the hall toward the front door, rubber. Neck stretch to the ceiling hands drag the floor her door closed he came together.

Good work, Charles, we're going to give you your own tree.

So there was the door. The mouthy wall gabbled on the floor water down the stream she sang winely there is a goon in my suit.

We know, Charles, you're afraid to go through the door.

29   THE DOORMAN

"No, I'm not. Porky on you, Mister Poopey!"

I'll just circle the crack. The airplane flew over with the mayor. Watch out CHARLES here comes the GIRL floating down the block see her with black stone hair nice she

"Hold on," said Charles. "This is a person." He pressed nose lips to the glass door.

Slip lacies and crack softlies she is going to come through the door CHARLES. You owe me four cents. Nice little shoes going sidewalk sidewalk

You'd like to get away, wouldn't you, she's almost here, carrying her books, don't get excited these are the best years of your life.

Take your nose away from the glass, maniac, she's coming through don't say anything to scare her.

"Boogle."

Look at the scarey person on her face

"Google. Boogle."

That's perfect, Charles, through the lobby she goes without eyes, fast away to the stairs.

I am a hanging around bad person, my teeth will fall out.

Well, it's time to go through the door.

Let's turn around three times to make sure. I hear dishes. Be careful, milky chicken, said Terrible Nobody.

Concentrate on the doorknob, please.

I can be there in forty-five years. All right, how about killing the driver.

Place your hand on the doorknob, Charles.

"Suppose I don't want to."

We'll let the baboons out of your crack we'll send Doctor Electric with his machine we'll kill you

"Help!"

Turn the knob, please.

HERE COMES THE MAILMAN

Nose lips pressed to glass. The door goes crrrk

"Hello, Mister Mailman."

"Hello, there."

"I opened the door for you."

"Yes, you did."

"Hello, Mister Mailman."

Mister Mailman has a pencil behind his ear. He makes the wall fall open. I am an old coloring book, a doggie scribbled on.

"Sure is a lot of mail, Mister Mailman."

"That's right."

"A million googies, I bet."

"Something like that."

The wall ate all the letters. I got a letter from my friend Nicky Jango.

You're lying, Charles.

"I'm not!"

There, the mailman heard, look at him looking.

Well, Nicky plays with me, you stinky voice, here comes his mother I'm afraid, Mrs. Jabootch, I don't think Charles and Nicky should play anymore.

"Well, so long," said the mailman.

Opening the door, Mister Mailman, closing the door, I am just an old colored man.

Get ready, Charles. Go get your clothes and all the things the dogs the dishes don't forget matches and let's go through this door, you're free

First, let's vote.

Get out of my way I'll open that door.

HERE COMES THE BEARDED MAN

In his beard stepping slowly down the sidewalk he comes forever he will say how's it going, man.

Charles the good opens the door for him.

"How's it going, man."

"They found a carrot in my brain."

"Sounds like a weird trip."

Down the bearded stone man goes down the hall all gone.

Well, it's about time Charles opened the door and went out in a white suit through the air

Sunlight crossed the door glass slowly. Charles watched ten thousand years.

Help I can't move!

"Charles, what are you doing here?"

Mommy lady held me someone's mommy voice behind

"You didn't go the store, did you?"

"I'm the doorman."

"Come upstairs, Charles. You're too sick to go the store today."

Today

The
Bird
Watcher

THE TREES GLISTENED in the morning sunlight as Twiller walked down the road with a pack on his back, singing

My heart sighs for you

Tootsie Rayder had sung that song at the junior high school talent show. She'd worn a low-cut gown, and at the last minute the guidance counselor made her cover up with a handkerchief but she won anyway.

My arms long for you
Please come back to me

Vincent Ferrara, the accordionist, had played *Lady of Spain*. Now he and Tootsie walked home from school together every day along the railroad tracks and it was said they performed the act in the abandoned switchman's shack. Twiller wished he could play the accordion instead of the clarinet, which honked whenever he blew in it.

He turned off the road onto the ballfield, climbed the right field fence and dropped down beside the smoking dump. It was the end of town.

Alongside the dump was an old grey house. Twiller walked to the rear of the house and down a flight of broken wooden steps. Knocking three times softly on the cellar door, he called, "Hello, Spider."

The window curtain parted for a moment, then closed, and the door opened.

"Come on in, man."

Twiller stepped into the underground kitchen of Spider Pronko. It was small, dark, and lopsided, with newspapers piled in the corners. Spider sat back down at a card table, where he was drinking a cup of black coffee. Twiller stood looking at a newspaper photograph pasted over the kitchen doorway. It was Spider's old man. He was in jail.

"Comin' tru." A voice came at Twiller from the dark bedroom and he stepped aside. Cleaning Lady Pronko came through in pink fur slippers. She had a face like a bulldog and knees like walnuts.

"Don'tchoo go no place wittout doin' dem dishes," she said, pointing to Spider's cup and saucer.

"Here, man." Spider threw his cup into the sink, where it shattered.

"The Boy Scout," said Cleaning Lady Pronko, slapping past them into the bathroom.

Spider walked into the bedroom and opened a bureau drawer.

"Should I bring the rod?"

"No," said Twiller. Spider's rod was a cap pistol with its chamber bored for real bullets. Gene Autry's face was on the handle and a thick rubber band was wound around it and over the hammer, giving it enough force to shoot a .22 caliber shell. When fired the bullets came out of the barrel sideways in a ball of flame. On their last camping trip Spider fired it into a pile of leaves and burned the woods down.

"Yeah, I'd better leave it," he said, closing the drawer, "I'm low on ammo." He went back to the kitchen and opened the refrigerator, taking out a bunch of bananas and a loaf of bread, which he dropped into a paper bag.

The bathroom door opened. Cleaning Lady Pronko stepped out and grabbed the bag from Spider. "Where you goin' wittat?"

"On a goddamn camping Boy Scout trip!" Spider grabbed the bag back and kicked the refrigerator door shut. A small plastic madonna trembled on top of the box. "Let's blow," he said. They went out the door and up the steps.

"When ya comin' back?" called Cleaning Lady Pronko.

Twiller turned to answer, but Spider took him by the elbow. "Just keep walkin', man."

They walked up the street and into a narrow alleyway, where they stopped at a small white house amongst the garages. "Crutch" Kane was waiting for them on the porch.

"Morning, fellas," he said, and swinging a pack onto his shoulders, limped down the stairs. He'd been run over by a beer truck several years back, and his right knee was the size of a grapefruit. His mother waved from the front door.

"Goodbye, Stanley."

"Goodbye, Stanley," mocked Spider Pronko, smudging Crutch's glasses with two fingers. Crutch's mother often used Cleaning Lady Pronko around the house.

They walked up the alley onto the brick avenue and marched along on the streetcar tracks, Spider singing

> *She jumped in bed*
> *And covered up her head*
> *And said I couldn't find her*
> *I knew damn well she lied like hell*
> *and I jumped in bed behind her*

Twiller and Crutch were wearing their Boy Scout uniforms. Spider wore a black sweat shirt and dungarees. The Scouts of Troop 7 were gathering at the end of the block in front of the old stone church. Spider ran into the crowd. Twiller and Crutch followed, slinging their packs against the wall of the church. A large man with braids on his shoulders and badges on his hat blew a whistle. The patrol leaders gave their commands:

"Beaver Patrol, fall in!"

"Flying Eagle Patrol, fall in!"

"Water Snake Patrol, fall in!"

"Fox Patrol, fall in!"

"Lone Wolf Patrol," said Twiller, "fall in!" Crutch Kane fell in. Spider Pronko was gone.

"Report your patrols," said Scoutmaster Ramsey, removing a notebook from his vest pocket.

"Beaver Patrol, all present and accounted for, sir!"

"Flying Eagle Patrol, all present and accounted for, sir!"

"Water Snake Patrol, all present and accounted for, sir!"

"Fox Patrol, all present and accounted for, sir!"

"Lone Wolf Patrol," said Twiller, "one man missing, sir."

"Where is he?"

"Latrine, sir."

"See that he gets in line. All right, fellows, stand by. We're loading the cars in a few minutes."

Twiller did not attempt to get Spider Pronko in line. Twiller had no advanced rank in the troop as he was unable to identify birds, and if he gave Spider the command to fall in, he might get punched out.

Mister Snow, the senior advisor of the troop, waved to Twiller and Crutch. "In this car, men." They picked up their gear and climbed into the back seat of his car. Mister Snow was an expert on birds and Twiller was afraid of him.

"Mister Snow was in the trenches," said Crutch, pointing to a medal hung on the dashboard. "Ever hear 'im talk?"

"No," said Twiller. Mister Snow was drill master of the troop. Twiller loved to drill and occasionally he won the weekly drill match, but Mister Snow never remembered his name.

"You hafta get 'im going," said Crutch.

The front door opened and Spider Pronko crawled in, carrying his paper bag. "We're shovin' out."

"Hey, Spider, gimme the old Boy Scout Handshake," said Crutch enthusiastically, holding out three fingers.

"Here, man." Spider gave him one finger.

Mister Snow climbed into the other side of the car and slipped behind the wheel. He put his hat on the seat and started the motor. "Very well, men, we're off."

With green flags waving from their car aerials, Troop 7 pulled onto the road and drove from the city into the wooded hills. The sun was rising over the mountain tops. A deer darted across the highway and stared at them from the trees.

Spider Pronko whispered into the back seat, "I shoulda brought the rod."

"Look," said Mister Snow, pointing out the window, "there's a red-hatted nuthatch."

Twiller looked. The trees went by in a blur. Beside the highway ran a sparkling river. Twiller watched the flashing water and thought about Tootsie Rayder. He'd never held a girl, except once when the troop gave a signaling demonstration at the Deaf and Dumb School and he'd danced with a girl who couldn't talk.

"Hey, Mister Snow," asked Crutch, "you were in the trenches, right?"

"That's right."

Spider sat up. "What kinda rod'ja have?"

"A revolver."

"Ever shoot anybody?"

"Listen," said Mister Snow. "That's a purple-throated gee-gaw. He says *geeble, geeble, geeble.*"

The river disappeared in the lowland as they climbed higher up the mountain. They rode for an hour, then turned off the highway and bounced down a dirt road into the forest. Scouts waved and cheered. Crutch shouted, "O.K., fellas!" and gave the Boy Scout Oath sign out the window. Twiller saw a lake gleaming through the trees.

"Here we are," said Mister Snow. They drove into a field, and parked alongside a large stone lodge in the trees. Twiller and Spider opened the doors and jumped out. Crutch followed and fell down.

"Careful, men," said Mister Snow.

"My knee fell asleep," said Crutch, crawling to his feet and saluting a tree.

Scoutmaster Ramsey blew his whistle.

"Lone Wolf Patrol, fall in!" said Twiller. Crutch Kane fell in. Spider Pronko was gone.

"Fellows," said Scoutmaster Ramsey, "we're here as guests of the lodge and I want a good clean camp."

Twiller saw an old woman in an apron standing on the front porch of the lodge. Behind a sunlit window on the second floor, he saw a face. It was Spider Pronko. Spider saluted the assembled troop with his middle finger and disappeared from the window.

"There's going to be a hike," said Scoutmaster Ramsey. "All those going on it meet at the footbridge behind the lodge. The rest of us will work on merit badges—cooking, signaling, and so forth. Choose your campsites carefully and don't set the woods on fire. Here are your bunk designations."

The Lone Wolf Patrol was assigned to the front porch. Twiller and Crutch carried their gear to the porch. Spider Pronko's paper bag was already there.

They stowed their gear and went into the lodge. Mister Snow was standing in front of a large stone fireplace, looking at the stuffed head of a doe.

"I smell food," said Crutch. They looked through a doorway, into a large kitchen. In front of the stove stood the old woman. Alongside her was a girl in tight blouse and faded blue jeans.

Crutch stuck his head through the doorway. "Hubba, hubba."

"Let's not collect around the kitchen, men," said Mister Snow.

Twiller and Crutch went out the back door of the lodge and caught sight of the girl through the kitchen window. "Boy," said Crutch, "I'd like to get her in my sleeping bag."

"Forget it," said Twiller. "One of the Eagle Scouts will get her."

"I can't forget," said Crutch. "I want to give her the Scout Handshake."

They walked into the field behind the lodge, and down to the footbridge, where the hikers were gathering with their packs. "Hiking eats it," said Crutch, limping toward the rippling stream.

Eagle Scout Billy Dalton, leader of the march, went among the hikers, adjusting their packs. "Not coming, Twiller?"

"No," said Twiller. Dalton had told him he had the stuff to become an Eagle Scout. At first Twiller had believed it, but now he knew he'd never make it. He'd been in the troop three years and his only merit badge was bookbinding.

"Hey," said Crutch, "a prisoner."

Scoutmaster Ramsey and Mister Snow came across the field with Spider Pronko marching bowleggedly between them. "Spider wants to go on the hike," said Scoutmaster Ramsey, turning Pronko over to Eagle Scout Dalton.

"Yes sir," said Dalton. "Fall in on the end, Pronko."

Spider fell in. Crutch gave Twiller the elbow. "Watch how long old Spider stays in line."

The troop bugler stepped onto the footbridge and blew *Begin-the-March.*

"Hey, man, blow that bugle up your ass," muttered Spider Pronko and the march began. The hikers crossed the footbridge and disappeared into the trees.

"Look," said Crutch.

The girl was standing in the back door of the lodge.

"Let's have a catch in the field," said Twiller. He could do some fancy pitching. She might see him from the doorway or the kitchen window.

"Naw," said Crutch, "baseball eats it."

Mister Snow came up behind them. "What merit badge are you men working on?"

"Bird-watching, sir," said Twiller.

"What is that bird on the limb right there?"

"Purple gee-gaw, sir."

"That is a chestnut-sided hong-wobbler."

"Yes sir."

"Carry on."

Twiller and Crutch saluted and walked along the edge of the field, peering into the trees for birds. They went past a rope-tying class in front of the lodge and on down the dirt road. When out of sight of the lodge, they ducked into the woods. Ahead of them through the trees was a small log cabin. They went quietly toward it and looked in the windows. Twiller pushed the door open and went in. The cabin was empty.

"Nobody's been here all year," said Twiller, stepping through spider webs. He climbed up a wooden ladder to the second floor of the cabin. Beneath the sloping roof was a small straw bunk, covered with dust.

"Hey, Crutch, it's nice up here."

"Yeah, I'm lookin' around down here."

Twiller lay on the bunk. "Be nice to bring somebody here."

"Yeah, your mother," said Crutch. "Let's go."

They went outside and walked down through the trees to the stream. Twiller jumped onto a rock in the middle of the rushing water. Crutch stood on the shore. From out of the woods darted the kitchen girl.

"Hubba, hubba!" said Crutch.

The girl stared at Twiller for a moment, then leapt from rock to rock across the stream. A bugle sounded through the trees. Spider Pronko and several scouts of the Snake Patrol dashed out of the woods.

Crutch gave the three-fingered Boy Scout salute. The girl disappeared over the river bank and Spider and the Snakes ran after her. Twiller jumped up the river bank and followed them into the woods. The girl was ahead, weaving through the trees. Twiller put on his speed and passed the Snakes, then pulled up beside Spider, whose wind was shot from smoking.

"Stop followin' me, man!" gasped Pronko.

Twiller passed him. The girl ran through a meadow and Twiller ran in after her. She was surefooted and fast and her long hair danced as she ran. Twiller raced through the bush, afraid to catch her.

She jumped a fallen tree and he followed, through bands of sunlight, into the tall pines. Down a grey avenue of trees they ran, feet falling softly on the needle floor. She stopped suddenly, turned, faced him.

He skidded to a halt. Her eyes were dark and she was smiling.

From behind them a Boy Scout jumped out of the grass, waving a pair of semaphore flags. The girl darted away. Out of the bush came a team of Signal Scouts, whooping and waving their flags overhead. Twiller was surrounded, then passed.

The girl was far ahead, running through a furrowed field. Twiller ran hard and passed the other scouts, coming up close behind her once again. She leapt a stone wall and Twiller leapt after her, followed by the Signal Scouts, flags waving.

"What's going on here, men?" Mister Snow was standing in the road with his compass reading class.

Twiller saluted. "Capture the Flag, sir." The girl was nowhere in sight.

"I thought it was bird-watching."

"Yes sir." Twiller saw Spider Pronko sneaking along the wall, up the road.

"What's your name?" asked Mister Snow, taking out his notebook.

"Twiller, sir."

"Twiller, I want no more foolishness from you. The woods are filled with birds."

"Yes sir."

"Carry on."

Twiller marched up the road. Once around the bend he began to run. The road wound through the forest and he ran along through the dust, heart pounding. The lodge came into view. He ran across the field and up the porch steps, into the living room. The kitchen door was locked. He put his ear to the keyhole. There was a sharp click behind him. He turned. A long thin switch blade was open at his throat.

"Stop followin' me, Boy Scout," said Spider Pronko.

At sunset the crickets began.

"If you count the seconds between their croaking," said Crutch, "you can figure out the temperature. I learned that from Scoutmaster Ramsey."

"What's the temperature?" asked Twiller.

"I get 110 degrees."

Night moths fluttered against the lighted windows of the lodge and flew in the door whenever it opened. The troop gathered around the fireplace singing

> O the deacon went down
> To the cellar to pray

Spider Pronko was in a corner, singing to the Snakes.

> O the moon shone bright
> On the nipple of her teat
> The wind blew up her nightie

The kitchen door opened. The girl came in wearing a buckskin jacket. She walked to the window beside the fireplace and raised her hips onto the sill. The singing around the fireplace grew more intense:

> He fell asleep
> And he slept all day
> I ain'na gonna grieve my Lord no more

and Spider harmonized quietly with the Snakes in the corner.

> *The sight I saw was against the law*
> *Jesus Christ Almighty*

With medals jingling on his chest, Eagle Scout Billy Dalton moved in beside the girl and offered her a toasted marshmallow on the end of a stick, which she accepted.

Twiller and Crutch pushed through the crowd to her side.

"Hubba, hubba," said Crutch.

"You run fast," said Twiller. She looked at him with a smile. An elbow stabbed him in the back.

"How's it goin', baby?" Spider Pronko moved in alongside her.

A bat squeaked down from the rafters. The troop let out a yell as it fluttered over their heads. Spider grabbed Twiller's campaign hat and leapt onto a table.

"Don't kill it!" shouted Mister Snow.

The bat circled the room. Spider swung the hat and the bat disappeared inside it. "Here you are, sir," said Spider, handing the hat over to Mister Snow.

The Scouts crowded around. The bat lay in the crown of the hat, its neck limp. "A fine thing," said Mister Snow, and walked out of the lodge with the hat in his hand.

Twiller turned back to the fireplace. The girl was gone.

Scoutmaster Ramsey blew his whistle. "Lights out, fellows."

Twiller ran onto the porch, looking for her. He saw a figure come out of the trees. It was Mister Snow.

"Excuse me, sir," said Twiller, stepping off the porch, "may I have my hat back?"

"We frightened him to death," said Mister Snow, and handing over the hat, walked past Twiller into the lodge.

Twiller looked inside the hat. All right, he thought, someone died in my hat. He put it on and walked to the back of the lodge, looking for her through the kitchen windows. It was dark and silent in the kitchen. He returned to the front of the lodge and stared into the trees. The sky was bright with moonlit clouds.

Crutch came up behind him. "Whattya see, a bear?"

Scoutmaster Ramsey walked onto the porch. "Let's have no trouble tonight, Twiller." During last year's campout, held on a local golf course, Twiller had been found sleepwalking in the sand trap.

"Yes sir," said Twiller. He felt himself rush into the trees to search for her, and stepped back onto the porch.

"You can bet some guys won't be sleepin'," said Crutch, unrolling his sleeping bag.

Twiller took off his hat and crawled into his bedroll. He felt light-headed and dizzy, as if he were floating out of his sleeping bag. A flashlight beam shined into his eyes.

"Where's Pronko?" asked Scoutmaster Ramsey, pointing the light on Spider's paper bag.

"Latrine, sir," said Twiller.

"See that he gets in line."

"Yes sir."

Twiller lay back down. One by one the flashlights and lanterns went out. He could hear logs falling in the fireplace. The camp was still.

"Look," whispered Crutch.

Something was moving on the other end of the porch. A dark figure crawled from bunk to bunk, then scurried past the door and slipped between Twiller and Crutch. It was Roscoe Benjamin, smallest Scout in the troop. "Spider gave her his knife," he whispered. "They're down in the cabin." He crawled off the porch and around the corner of the lodge.

Twiller lay staring at the moon. He slipped out of his sleeping bag and walked quietly through the lodge doorway, stepping over sleeping bags until he found Mister Snow on the floor in front of the fireplace. He tugged gently on the old man's bedroll. Mister Snow turned over.

"Yes?"

"Sir, I don't feel so good."

"What's wrong? Do you have to go the bathroom?"

"No sir."

"Just a minute," said Mister Snow, "we don't want to wake the others." He crawled out of his sleeping bag and they walked onto the porch.

"What is it?" asked Mister Snow.

"I feel like I'm falling," said Twiller.

"You say you fell?"

"No sir."

"You don't hurt anywhere?"

"No sir."

"Go back to sleep, my boy," said Mister Snow, patting him on the shoulder. "It was just a dream."

The
Jewel
of
Amitaba

VEILED ONLY by her long black hair, and a necklace of
elbow macaroni, Adria La Spina, the beautiful pasta
heiress, snaked her hips to electric guitars, while the
paparazzi shot their flashbulbs off around her. Notable
among the photojournalists was Norton Blue, the celebrated
pornographer, with his sensitive Polaroid.

"Let's have a shot of your eggplant, my dear!" shouted
the depraved Blue, scuttling on his knees across the patio, in
a cardboard nose.

La Spina villa was built on the rolling Roman hills, its
balconies overlooking the ruins of antiquity. Music and
laughter filled the estate, and several squat ladies in black,

whose custom for years had been to pass the quiet groves of
La Spina on the way to market, peered pop-eyed through
the gates at the young pasta heiress, who by now had shed
her macaroni necklace and danced *tutta nuda* through the
trees.

"*Prostituta!*" shouted one of the women, and tearing a
length of pepperoni from her shopping bag, shook it
through the iron gates.

A large Doberman pinscher flashed across the lawn and
ripped the pepperoni from her grasp, devouring it just
beyond her reach, his fierce little eyes on her all the while.

"*O–O–Diavolo!*" sputtered the woman, and marched off to
report the disgrace of La Spina to Monsignor Farina,
prelate of the local parish.

"O.K., fellas, hit it!" Jeekers Peltz, derelict leader of
"Jeekers and the Stools," gave the downbeat. Several
seconds later the hallucinatory music of his filthy untrained
group shattered the stillness which had briefly surrounded
La Spina during lunch, and the savage chaos of the number
woke the house-guests from their afternoon slumber.

Hedvig von Cuckle, daughter of German Chancellor
Weiner von Cuckle, splashed into the rose-marble fountain,
clad only in a brass chain given her by the American
hoodlum Bad Mother Hole, who slept mouth open on his
motorcycle near poolside, a Nazi helmet over his eyes;
beautiful Luisa Pina-Bodega came riding across the lawns
of La Spina on an irredeemable Cuban donkey famous for
a decadent nightclub act in old Havana; Lieutenant
Colonel Miriam Boombeh, on leave from the Israeli
Defense Force, was in her plain army underwear, teaching

hand-to-hand combat to the paparazzi. All over La Spina, guests were stirring, led by Adria La Spina, upon the front balcony, shaking first one hip, then the other, up and around in devastating rhythm, as Jeekers and the Stools went slowly deaf on the patio.

"More porn, my dear!" shouted Norton Blue, his face flushed with intoxicants. He was in a refined Royal Canadian Exercise Corps posture, flat on his back on the patio, a bottle of Canadian Club balanced on his forehead. Beside him in a deck chair was Cojones Colada, the jackbooted Cuban revolutionary, who had managed to stop his powerful '59 Studebaker outside the gates of La Spina.

"I knew a woman whose breasts were shaped like bananas," said Blue. "You would have liked her."

"Jes, jes," said Colada.

"She was a melancholy creature, of course," said Blue, sipping from his bottle.

"Gentlemen," said Duval, the French philosopher, joining the group at poolside, the usual licorice pipe in his mouth, and sharing, as was his habit, a trench coat with his mother.

"I am searching," said Blue, raising his head, "for the lady with three breasts. I glimpsed her once in a dream. She had a third moon on her neck."

Madame Duval made a puzzled face. "Surely, a goiter . . ."

"Madame, a man in my execrable profession does not mistake such detail." Blue struggled to raise himself on his elbow. "If I had such a woman, I could topple a banana republic, install myself as *presidente*, wear an ice cream vendor's uniform, eh, Colada?"

"Jes, jes," said Colada, not listening. His eyes were on Adria coming toward them, for she wore only an old railroader's handkerchief tied loosely around her caboose.

With her was grape drink king Sophocles Trismegistus, gesticulating. He had named an orchard after Adria, but had yet to squeeze her pear. "I am a small celebration for my daughter giving," said Trismegistus, as they approached the poolside group. "She has reach the age of consequence. I was wonder," he said, touching Adria's wrist, "if you pleasure us by attendance."

"Sorry," said Adria, "I don't like society balls."

"*Señorita, por favor,*" said Cojones Colada, standing and extending his chair, his hawk-eyes bulging. The previous evening she had refused his celebrated sugar cane.

The crumbling opium smuggler G appeared spectrally at poolside, like a cloud out of the blue water. Opening a pearl case, he handed thin gold-tipped cigarettes around to the guests.

"Ah," said Blue, as a wreath of pungent smoke encircled the group, "you have recently returned from Tangier."

"When I was a little girl . . ." said Adria, smoking dreamily. She slipped down in her chair. Her gently rounded belly lifted to the blue southern sky and she closed her eyes. The years fell away. She was a little girl in the kitchen. Uncle Dido had come for Sunday breakfast after Church. They were alone. *Show me your woo-woo,* said Uncle Dido. *I give you chocolate.* She stood in the sunlight. A crystal bowl glittered on the table. Uncle Dido put on his Micka da Mouse mask, and crawled beneath the table.

"*Señorita,* how you like hob of Prime Miniskir of Cuba?"

The voice of Cojones Colada shattered the glass bowl, the memory faded. Adria stood.

"I am going to the East."

The silver-jetted bird rose into the sky. By strange coincidence, sitting beside Adria in first class was Sebastian Cloud, the *enfant terrible* of Europe at the time, dressed as the Archbishop of Canterbury.

"Might I interest you in a sacrament?" he said, and before a thousand miles were gone, Adria and he were deep in ecumenical embrace.

The lights of the Japanese islands appeared and they came down in Tokyo at midnight. They roamed the streets of the great city, played the pinball machine, fed the rooster of good luck. In the temple of Buddha Amitaba, Sebastian, pretending prayer, popped the jewel from the idol's forehead into his tall miter hat.

At dawn they walked along Tokyo Bay among the fishmongers, Sebastian tapping the street with his crooked staff.

"What say we get married? I'll perform the ceremony." A basket of squid was before them, squirming with tentacles.

"If you'll take me away," said Adria.

"I propose the Amazon," said Sebastian, lifting a squid on the end of his shepherd's crook. "Missionaries are desperately needed there."

"No touch!" screamed the fishseller, pointing at the hanging squid with a chopping knife.

"Quiet, my man, or I shall baptize you. Well?" asked Sebastian, handing Adria the jewel from Amitaba's forehead.

"Yes," said Adria, "let's go today."

An hour before flight time, they went to the Jade Bathhouse, were separated in the steam, and never saw each other again.

Exceedingly depressed, Adria wandered the city alone. At evening, she stood upon the wooden bridge crossing the stream Otukisama, Goddess of the Moon. Exquisite memories of Sebastian filled her with despair, and she wept quietly, clutching the wedding jewel he'd given her.

A frog was singing devoutly to the sunset, and Adria tried to lose herself in his song. She stared at the water, in which the suspended red drum of the setting sun was reflected. The spirit of silence stole over her, but *let us be going, on and on,* said her restless heart. Yet she remained still, and suddenly her thoughts were gone, swallowed by the moonstream.

Beneath its surface she saw waving weeds, like gold ropes tying the sun which floated like a golden flower. Suddenly the flower opened and in its center sat a gold being.

Radiant snakes danced at his feet, and one, a brilliant coral, slipped into Adria, piercing her along the spine. *He is Buddha Amitaba, Lord of the Western Paradise,* sang the snake. Quivering, Adria sank to her knees.

The Buddha came forth from the flower throne. His eyes were blue lapis lazuli, in which gold banners flew in flickering expression. A nimbus of many colors surrounded his head, and as he stepped toward her, red and blue balls appeared beneath his feet, in molecular pattern.

The elegant creature wrapped a glowing patchwork cloak around his shoulders, circumambulated Adria thrice and disappeared into the infinity of space, leaving her with a deafening silence in her heart.

For days she wandered the streets of Tokyo, neither eating nor sleeping, sustained by her encounter with the powerful being. Gradually, however, the feeling subsided, and to regain it, she climbed Fujicamat Mountain, to a Zen monastery, and prostrated herself before the Master.

"Accept me in the order."

"No good," said the Master. Several young monks had gathered around wide-eyed, and the noon bell was clumsily struck.

"Please," begged Adria.

"Why you grow such big breasts?" said the Master, and striking Adria on the backside with a stick, drove her out of the monastery gate.

A Tokyo camera club which had followed Adria up the mountain leapt out of the bushes, and cheering, picked her up out of the dust.

"A wet bag of bones!" shouted the Master, and slamming shut the gate, returned to his archery practice, the shooting of a rice cake off his own head.

The camera club wound its way back down the mountain, carrying Adria like a goddess, in a bamboo palanquin. Her old ways, she realized, were impossible to escape, and she obliged the cameramen with several interesting shots of her eggroll.

Into the sun on Japan Airlines flew the pasta heiress, on the second lap of her journey. By strange coincidence, she shared a seat with the renowned sitarist, Ali Clarkbar. She told him how much she enjoyed his playing, and he must have enjoyed her too, for when they disembarked from the plane at Bengali, the guru's knees were trembling and Adria's mumu was on backward.

They stood on the blazing airstrip, gazing deeply into each other's eyes. Clarkbar laid his thumb upon her forehead, between her brows. "Beware of false swamis," he said, and departed.

The advice was wasted on romantic Adria, who quickly fell in with magicians. Soon she was leaving her body at night on plunges to the heart of the earth, where she danced in dreams of red and green, adorned in luminous macaroni. The violent nature of the handsome demons excited her fancy, and they were not adverse to burying their thunderbolts in her mortal coil.

When her visa expired, however, Adria was tired of witchery, and wanted to go home, to the lawns of La Spina, to its familiar walls and gardens. To the beat of a dark drum, slapped in the moonlight by black hands, she boarded an Air India coach. By strange coincidence, her traveling companion was the distinguished psychologist, Doctor B. F. Goodreich. Moonlight gleamed on the swept wing. Adria told him of her vision on Otukisama Bridge.

"Amitaba is a projection," said the exalted physician. "That is to say, my dear young lady, you are Amitaba."

Norton Blue and his double-dyed crew were waiting for Adria at Roma International Airport, blowing paper snakes. At the sight of Blue's head, on which a Bulgarian postmark was tattooed, Adria burst into tears.

The depraved band boarded a rented limousine and drove to La Spina, where a welcome party for Adria had been going five days. Music and laughter filled the air, and exotic slide shows designed by the master, Blue himself, flickered in several rooms, featuring the degraded Brazilian café star, Captain Diez y Ocho and his defiled gorilla.

Blue showed Adria to the kitchen, where a wizened oriental in ceremonial robe was supervising the preparation of meals.

"In view of your Eastern trip," said Blue, "I took the liberty of hiring Fat Tong here. He is a disciple of D. T. Yumabachi, the Macaroniotic Master. Yumabachi, as you may recall, ate but a single macaroni a day boiled in dog's milk, slept standing up in a cupboard and lived to the remarkable age of twenty-seven. Delicious," said Blue, taking a spoon of soup.

In the third week of the party, Monsignor Farina visited Adria secretly in the night by the rose trellis outside her balcony.

"*Signora*," said the priest, waving a smoking censer, "you must be more discreet."

"Father," said Adria, "the old ways are gone."

There was a knock at her door. The prelate quickly crawled down the trellis to the ground.

The paparazzi, led by Blue, leapt out of the bushes with their cameras.

"Back, back!" cried Monsignor Farina, waving a sprig of garlic in the air.

Eyes watering, unable to focus, Blue cringed. Monsignor Farina fled out the gate, chased by the dogs, his bald head shining like a poached egg in the moonlight.

The paparazzi revived Blue with brandy. He sat up, saw Adria on the balcony in her pale dressing gown.

"What do you suppose accounts for their firmness, gentlemen," said Blue, pointing to Adria's heaving bosom, "hormone cream in her *cannoli,* perhaps?"

The paparazzi lifted him up, adjusted his electric tie. "I must go to her," said Blue, and taking hold of the trellis, ascended to the balcony.

"Will you marry me?" he asked, clinging to the railing.

Adria looked at him, did not speak.

"We might have a small ceremony," said Blue, "you in a rubber gown, I in a chicken suit . . ."

"Norton," said Adria in a whisper, her fingers moving over the jewel of Amitaba which she wore around her neck.

"Yes, my dear?"

She put her arm through Blue's. Turning him toward the western sky, she pointed to the dark horse nebula. "I belong to one out there," she said.

Blue held a small plastic viewer to his eye, pointing it at the moon. "Peculiar posture this woman is in, look here—"

"He's very old," said Adria, "and has united himself with—"

"—with a seeing-eye dog, it's an extraordinary pose—"

"—with the principle of nature," said Adria.

"Here," said Blue, handing her the little viewer, "when you turn this wheel, the dog sits up and begs." He let go of the balustrade and climbed slowly down the trellis to the ground.

Spring came; Adria went out to enjoy the gentle wind blowing on the hills. The sun was climbing behind La Spina. For a moment it seemed to balance on the crest of a hill, and out of the glaring disc stepped a figure, walking down the wooded path alongside the estate.

At first, Adria thought he was dancing, then she saw a hapless spastic, whose walk was that of a tangled puppet, manipulated by a fiend. He was a shrunken wretch, and carried a small seabag on his shoulders. His arms seemed hidden somewhere up behind his back, but then Adria saw he had no arms at all, only little hands, like flippers, growing out of his shoulders. He wore a sailor's blue watch cap, and as he walked, whistled through fish-lips, a senseless tune.

Agog, Adria feasted her eyes on famine. The little man's head was off-center, permanently turned several degrees to the right, so that he appeared to walk sideways in drunken fandango. He flopped by her, but she could not see his face, for his neck was buckled toward the other side of the path.

Circling gulls jeered at him. What did he care, he was born in a bone warp. Below were the olive trees, ahead the horizon, his goal the waterfront, for he was a wharf rat, and hung like floatsam by docks and piers, crouching for a bone from the ship's mess, hoping to be shanghaied and drowned. His chest was collapsed; hunf-tweet he breathed and flung himself on, past the villa, making to go forward his monstrousness, snort, snort.

Adria maneuvered in front of him. The sun was behind her dragon gown and her luxurious curves were apparent. The wharf rat's miserable left eye was focused up the road, but his right was obliquely upon her; pure symmetry terrified him, and he steered his wreck past her, averting his gazes.

"Please," said Adria, and stepping around him, looked

into his face. It was a gargoyle, with temples bloated like a hammerhead shark; he had no eyebrows and his nose was a baboon's. His skin was sick and prickly as a plucked chicken. In human traffic, he was a monster. What archetype inspired his existence, to what class of being he was avatar of beauty, cannot be known by a groping mortal. Yet something in Adria responded, some frimpish bugle in her own spirit blew at the sight of the fluke, for she groped his rope belt, trying to detain His Monstrosity for lunch at La Spina.

The little ugliness struggled up the path, dragging her behind him. His twisted legs were strong, but his wind was short, and he weakened.

"Come with me," said Adria, "I'll give you something to eat," and she maneuvered him into the flower gardens of La Spina, down the stone walkway, to the marble pool given her in a moment of supreme indiscretion by United States Senator Sparrow Bowlwater, who had attempted to snorkel her at a health spa. The pool was shaped like a cowboy boot; the stupefied spastic sat on the toe, barking for air.

"Darling," said Adria, massaging the muscles of his neck, a sailor's nightmare of knots.

He looked at her suspiciously out of the corner of his toad-eye, then pointed to his reflection in the water.

"Yes, beloved," said Adria. She fingered the buttons on his ragged middy blouse, and finally removed it, unveiling a lizard-scale skin with odd clumps of hair and the duck-like flappers which grew out of each shoulder.

"May I get comfortable?" asked Adria, and removed her gown, pressing a breast into his fin-fingers. He fondled it abstractly. She encircled him from behind with her legs but in her passion went too far, and the duck-man tumbled forward into the pool. He flapped his fins for a moment, then sank.

Adria dove after him. He sat on the bottom, a hideous blowfish, bubbles rising from his mouth. She clutched his belt and brought him to the surface, shoving him onto the patio where he lay, flopping.

She applied pressure to his warped seachest. Gasping, he opened his eyes.

"Yes, darling, you need air," said Adria, and with some difficulty removed the trousers off his corkscrew legs. The mock-sailor lay naked, then, and she beheld his precious cargo—a mouse's sack and a rat's tail.

Out of the bushes stepped the deteriorate Blue, quietly motioning his cameramen into position. They fixed tripods, read the light.

Adria lowered herself slowly onto the little sea urchin, slipping his cargo into her hold.

The cameras began grinding. "Oh, god," moaned Adria, and cast off, rowing gently, up and down.

"Arf, arf," said the wharf rat, in diverse spasm, making signals with his flippers, legs twitching.

"Down, darling," said Adria, shaking her poopdeck, "take me . . . down stream."

"A mystical invocation," said Blue, "are we running sound?"

"*Definitivamente, signore.*"

Adria felt waves breaking around her, heard the roaring of surf.

"Arf!" sang the duckman, staring at the sky.

"Curious tongue," said Blue, "get a boom mike in there."

The waves tossed Adria up, then let her down, and the wharf rat's oar sank deep into her salty lagoon. She closed her eyes, saw the blue ocean and floating upon it, a stink-weed bud. The waves broke around it, stirring its homely petals. She squeezed her thighs together, locking the dwarf-sailor's oar. The stink-weed flower turned in a whirlpool, opening slowly.

"Darling," groaned Adria, quivering on the mainmast, "I'm sinking . . ."

"Arf!"

"Sink me, sink me!" cried Adria, as the waves rushed in, warm and bright, drowning her.

"Arf, arf!"

The stink-weed opened; in it sat a thousand-finned seaman, with jeweled hammer-head, frog-eyes glowing like pearls. *I am a traveler,* he whispered, and exploded into a thousand seamen, and they sailed down the foaming crest to the cove.

"Adria," said Blue, "cheat your head a little to the right, that's it, darling. Camera One, close up on that."

Adria bathed her lover at poolside, cooing like a seabird in his webbed ears. Tenderly, she buttoned him into his trousers and slipped the middy blouse over his head.

The wharf rat stood before her in his little blue hat. She removed from around her neck the jewel of Amitaba and gave it to him along with a macaroni sandwich. He put them in his seabag. Then, bending over, he picked up a small round stone in his flipper and handed it to her. Shouldering his bag, he flopped out the gate and struggled down the path, toward the farther valley, without looking back.

Adria went after him. "No, my dear," said Blue, restraining her, "you can't keep him here."

"I must," said Adria, weeping. "He is Amitaba," but as she spoke a veil fell away from the day and she saw all around her the face of Amitaba, hideously beautiful, sublimely twisted, written in the leaves, the gates, the road, in Norton Blue's electric tie.

"All right, gentlemen," said Blue, signaling to his camera crew, "wrap it up. I should like to be in the gutter before sunset."

Nippy

HE WAS a low cur, born of the streets, descended from so
many lines of body, bone and blood that he was nearly not
a dog at all, but seemed to represent a nether region of the
species, some exiled post on the last receding ledge of the
canine family, beneath which there was only the dark
domain of the rodent, to whom he bore a remarkable
resemblance.

His name was Nippy for he had teeth as sharp as needles
and biting people was his first love, though he was also fond
of chewing shoes and table legs.

We shared my room, but that was all we shared, for
Nippy could not be trained or trusted. He would not sit up,

roll over, or be a watch dog; he watched only for a chance to escape, and if he got out of the house without his leash, ran straight for the garbage dump.

On a leash, he would bite anyone he came near, with a preference for the tender white meat on the leg of our neighborhood priest, though he would settle for the dark meat on the priest's housekeeper.

The rest of the walk he spent winding the leash around a tree, under a fence, or into some bushes, forcing me to release my grip or be blinded by pickers. Off he would go, chasing some dark fugitive scent, the leash trailing behind him.

Perhaps our closest moments were those spent in the chase, for they are the only ones I remember clearly— running down grey alleyways in the afternoon, between buildings, over fences, off of walls, Nippy plunging into space, with me behind him.

Finally, he went too far. Mother, Father, and I had gone away for the weekend, leaving Nippy locked in my room with a bowl of food and water. When we returned, I ran straight to my room to see my little friend.

The room was covered with feathers. Nippy had pulled the pillow off my bed and dragged it around the room, shaking it in his teeth no doubt, like a soft white goose he had by the throat, slamming it up and down on the floor until it lay limp and empty, its feathers spreading in a mist which had settled over everything in sight.

Lying on the floor was a tall wooden clothes tree he'd managed to topple after leaving some dark wet stains on its carved claw feet. My father's fishing hat, which had hung on the tree, was in the middle of the room, ripped to shreds, like a murdered bird.

"What did you do?" yelled my mother, waving her finger in Nippy's face, which I quickly covered with my own.

"What did you do here?" shouted my father, picking up his battered hat and chasing Nippy around the room with it, landing several loud slaps on the dog's bony brown behind, as the mist of dancing feathers was swept into the air.

"Who did *this*?" yelled my mother, blowing feathers from her nose and mouth, and pointing to a malodorous deposit Nippy had made, not on the newspapers which she and I had so carefully laid down for him, but on my game linoleum, right in Little Miss Muffet's lap.

My father opened the back door to sweep out the feathers, and Nippy darted out between his legs.

"Let him go," said my father. "If he wants to go, let him go."

I went after him, but he'd gotten older and wiser, especially to the ways of the alley. He was far ahead, free and going farther, without a leash, without a collar, without a thing of ours but his name.

"Come back, Nippy!" I cried, but he didn't look back. The day was grey and the wind strong, with something irresistible in it, a wild smell blowing up from the underworld.

He turned a corner far away, and when I turned it after him, he was already into the garbage dump, racing down the dusty road, through the smoldering trash, into the world of the rats.

I ran along in the junk, to where the road bent down to a

great shelf of trash, and sighted him bounding over the tin cans, headed for the woods beyond the dump.

In those woods, the hobos lived; sometimes you'd hear of a girl going in there with young men for dark pleasures, and into these woods Nippy plunged, through the large weed leaves, seeking his own sinister joys.

I had nothing to offer him, standing in my short pants and suspenders, peering across the smoking dump into the forbidden wood. He was older than me, a thousand years older, an old dog of ancient ruin, going, gone.

Elephant
Bangs
Train

Reuters News Service
Nairobi, Kenya May 25, 1969

YELLOW FLOWERS on the hillside tempted him upward. He
climbed the green slope, pulling the flowers up with his
trunk and swallowing them down. The herds were grazing
and there were no screams. The cats had hunted and eaten
in the coolness before dawn and were sleeping now on the
sunlit cliffs. The elephant's custom was to eat from sunup to
sundown, and he tossed his tail happily, for the yellow
flowers were exceptional.

He nibbled his way onto a plateau, where a peculiar path
appeared, wide and covered with stones, like a river-bed.
The flowers grew between the stones and he ate his way

along the strange path, wondering what animal made use of it. On either side of the path was a shining bone, hot, with unfamiliar scent, curving through the trees. Never had he seen anything like it in his own part of the jungle.

He had wandered far from the herd, on the trail of greener leaves, and dark-winged birds of death circled in the sky of the unknown land, but he was not anxious. He had dealt with the leopard and impaled the sleek cheetah. With the lion, there had never been dispute, for it was not good for kings to quarrel. He continued down the path, consuming flowers and grass.

Suddenly the monkeys began to chatter, as when a big cat reveals himself and races through the grass. The antelope scattered on the plain. The elephant stopped eating and heard, far off, the roar which had frightened the antelope. It was like many elephants running, but he could distinguish no familiar voice. He returned to his eating, with ears forward, and one eye to the trees. The ground began to tremble, and he continued to eat, with no further pleasure, the yellow flowers.

He saw a great shadow slip through the distant trees. It seemed like many, yet he saw only one body, moving fast. Black dust flew in the air above the treetops, and the monkeys cried *Run!* Were he not of noble breed, he might have done so. Indeed, were he a dog or jackal there would be no issue. Since he was a king there was no question. He remained on the path and watched the long shadow advancing.

Bright and glistening, with many teeth, a great swift serpent came out of the trees. He faced it, ready to debate over territory. It was dark-headed, with cold, expressionless eye, and lashed an enormous tail.

Slowly it came toward him, and he blew an introductory note of warning, but it was lost in the hiss of the great snake. Almost atop him, it swallowed up the bones and flowers on the path, and screamed for him to stand aside. His ears twitched with pain from the scream, but he did not move, for the thousand eyes of the jungle were upon him.

The serpent pushed him, and roaring with anger, he pushed back, but the stones slid beneath his feet. He slipped backward, and the sharp cold teeth of the serpent came between his legs, knocking him off balance. He struggled to hold on to the serpent with his trunk, but his legs were pushed from underneath him. The ground slipped away, he fell, and bleating furiously, tumbled down the hill.

Dumbfounded at the outrage, he struggled to his feet. The serpent passed without further attack. Its tail clicked triumphantly, and its harsh scent filled the air, burning his nose.

The monkeys chattered and the parrots talked. He hurried away to the open plain, trying to escape their comment, but the laughter of the jackal pursued him through the high grass, and on a distant cliff, the lion roared disdainfully.

He walked to the river, to submerge and put the taunts of the jungle out of his ears. He stepped into the water, and a hippo surfaced in front of him, sleepy mockery in her eyes.

On the fierce lips of the monkeys, his humiliation passed through the trees. Their insane chattering was everywhere. He called for silence but they swung above his head, out of reach, gibbering viciously. His ears burned, and he longed for nightfall, when the dark cats would hunt, and none would be quick to speak.

He walked, head down, through the green land, toward the cliffs, a mistake, for the baboons were there, howling and nodding to each other. He did not reply to their insults, for whatever was said to a baboon was hurled back like rotten fruit.

He entered a dark grove of trees, and nibbling unhappily on the leaves, pondered his problem. With the entire jungle singing his shame, he could not return to his herd.

He might do better to walk off the edge of a cliff, and let the death dogs have his body. He sampled a small white flower. There was no need to be hasty. Certain delicacies were still for the taking.

The breeze turned and he caught a familiar, enriching smell through the leaves. He listened quietly, then called softly. The leaves rustled and the smell enveloped him. He moved the branches aside with his trunk.

There stood a beautiful cow. Her eyes spoke many encounters; a great swelling began between his haunches. He circled her, to get behind and mount, but she turned her tail away from him with express denial. He playfully offered her his trunk, but she refused it. He raised up on his back legs and blew a sweet note, but she did not move, and the look in her eyes cut through him like the claws of a cat. His disgrace was already a legend. She shuffled away from him, into the forest.

The great swelling between his haunches was not relieved. The baboons suggested he insert it in a mud bank. Bellowing with rage, he shook the trees with his trunk, tearing their roots, and the baboons leapt away, howling with laughter.

He stood defeated in the dismal grove. What cow would have him now? An old cow, perhaps, with bumps on her head, was the best he could hope for. Then, from faraway, he heard a familiar sound.

He listened as it grew louder, and his rage mounted slowly from tail to trunk. He moved quickly through the trees onto the plain. There, in the bed of grass, he saw the strange path once again, and the long shining bones, and in the distance, the great shadow slithering through the trees.

The light was fading and the day had grown cooler. The ground trembled and the rumbling grew louder. A dark cloud streamed in the sky, and circling above it were the birds of death. The serpent came out of the forest and onto the plain, its bright eye shining.

He trotted toward it, until the serpent's head was fully exposed, and then he charged. The plain blurred, and he closed in with head down.

The serpent saw him and screamed, but his rage was full and he rammed it directly. Darkness fell and cats' eyes glistened; the serpent shuddered and gave way. He hooked it in the belly with his tusks and drove it off the path. The serpent screeched, lashing its tail. He backed away dizzily, his head throbbing, and charged once more, burying his tusk in the serpent's eye.

The serpent did not move. He had killed it. He sounded his triumph and walked away with deliberate slowness. He heard angry voices, like those of the baboons, cursing him, but he did not recognize the tongue, and did not care. The dark-eyed cow was waiting in the trees, and as he came toward her, she turned slowly and showed him her haunches.

The
Magician

The magician stood in the alley outside the cabaret, breathing the night air. Under the light of the stage door sat his wife, sewing a silver button on his evening jacket. A sturdy, buxom woman, she cut the thread with her strong teeth, then stood and held the jacket out.

The magician turned and stepped toward her lightly, a magician's walk, pointed-toed across the stones, through the mist rolling in from the river, as a ship edging out to sea sounded its mournful horn.

"The horns of Tibet," said the magician. "You hear them down the mountain passes, invoking the Buddha."

"Yes, darling," said his wife, holding out his jacket, smiling patiently.

The night is hypnosis, he thought, not daring to look in her eyes, for he would go tumbling into them. From within the cabaret came the sound of a trumpet; in the stage doorway his wife's eyes were wickedly bright, and he could not resist.

"Please, darling," she said, for he hadn't much time before his act, but she let him fall, until she could feel him inside her, rummaging around in her old loves, her flown and tattered past. What a strange one he was, always exploring around inside her with those eyes of his, peering into the dear dead days of a woman. It was bizarre play, but she let him, for some men demanded much more, and it was more painful in the giving. That was the way of the waterfront, where strange men came ashore. Into their arms she'd fallen, for she loved a sea story, and their dark songs. But then along he'd come, the top-hatted magic one, and she had said so here you are at last, which was all a magician needed, some portentous note to thrill him for an age or two. So they'd married, and he was still looking around inside her, and he has plenty more to see, she thought, before he grows tired.

She broke the spell, waving his jacket at him. He turned gracefully, plunging his arms into the sleeves, noticing at the same moment a wandering couple coming out of the mist on the avenue—an elderly man in evening dress, singing to himself, on his arm a young woman in high-collared cape, with her hair cut short, like a boy. As the lights of the cabaret appeared to them, the young girl began to plead, "Oh, may we stop here? They have a magic show!"

"Yes, yes," said the old fellow, continuing on, in deep tremolo, his song, *"O du Liebe meiner Liebe . . ."*

The magician watched them move out of the lamplight and pass under the awning of the cabaret.

"Yes," said the magician's wife, handing him his top hat, "she's very beautiful."

"Now, my dear," said the magician with a laugh, "you know me better than that." He tapped his hat and kissed her on the forehead. Women were so quick to suspect a man it made one blush. "Come, old girl," he said, giving her his arm, "I feel a good show brewing."

The dancing girls kicked their bare legs in the glow of the footlights, scattering balloons over the smoky stage, then disappeared into the wings amid applause and the rattle of dishes. Three drunken pit musicians struck up a tinny fanfare; one of the dancing girls returned, holding a gilt-edged sign bearing the magician's legend.

His wife kissed him on the cheek and he made his entrance, coming out onto the stage from the wings. Removing his white gloves and top hat, he signaled to the light bridge.

A spotlight swept through the audience, illuminating the tables, and at the magician's direction stopped amid a setting of sparkling wine goblets and dessert dishes, on the table of an elderly man in evening dress. His companion, a young woman, tried to withdraw from the smoky beam. The magician came to the edge of the stage.

"Please," he said, holding out his hand, "will you assist me?"

Seeing the girl's reluctance, the audience began to clap. Her escort helped her from her seat. She walked toward the stage, smiling nervously. In her short-cropped hair and cape she looked like a beautiful schoolboy.

The hypnosis began slowly; the magician asked her questions, relaxing her with small talk, at the same time flashing in her face the brilliant stone from his ring, playing its reflection over her eyes like a miniature spotlight.

They stood in the middle of the stage, he smiling confidently, she looking fearfully into his fierce, piercing fox-eyes. She would not let herself be hypnotized, that was that, she would resist.

He stepped closer to her, touching her wrist lightly with his fingers. Her face was purple in the spotlight, her dark eyes like windows, and he could not resist slipping through them, into her hidden dimension.

The center of his forehead tingling, he passed through the delicate veil; there was her youth and its tender longing, there her childhood and its delight, here her infancy in white, and finally the darkness of the womb in which she had slept. He started to surface, then saw a light in the darkness, and he plunged through this still more delicate veil, into her most secret self. Down he went, through the gloomy ruins, where her antique past was kept, and long-dead shadows chased.

Standing still as a stone on the stage, the young woman heard distant voices, as if calling across the water.

Something had happened, a magic show, how odd she felt, as if in a dream.

Through the labyrinth he tracked, into the depths of her soul, where her spirit was hidden away in its meditation. As in the rooms of a museum, he passed the relics of her former lives—a nun's veil, a gladiator's net, a beggar's tin cup.

Suddenly a figure appeared, a priestess, highborn, by the sea, of luminous and beautiful body, in the hallway of a temple hauntingly familiar to him. In gold-braided sandals and a necklace of shells she walked by the sea and he who walked beside her . . .

The young woman and the magician stood motionless on the smoke-filled stage, she floating on the waves of the trance, he agasp with a recollection.

"I loved you on Atlantis," he said with trembling voice.

Instantly the waves enveloped her, her mind swam, she was under. There was a city with waving banners. She stood inside an ocean shell and felt the water on her feet. How sweet it was upon the beach and he who danced upon the waves . . .

No, he thought, pulling back from her, but he could not stop his descent, for they were ancient lovers.

A thousand lives have I loved you, she said, seeing clearly in the mirror of her heart the chain of their love.

Struggling in the tidal wave, he turned to the audience. "Now, ladies and gentlemen, tonight I would like to perform for you a most daring feat of magic!" With trembling hands, he lifted the girl and placed her between two chairs. She lay stretched out in the air, stiff as a board.

She saw now, worlds were tucked within worlds, memory was vast. She came down a river and there on its banks she saw him dancing in a loose gown. She lay in the river on stones as omens reared in the sky—a procession of elephants in gold harness, and he, dancing, brown-skinned, an African prince.

"Now then," said the magician, snapping his fingers, "bring on the box." He held to the edge of a chair, trying to pull himself together.

Two of the dancing girls came out, carrying a large wooden box, which they placed between a pair of sawhorses.

"The subject is in deep trance," said the magician, raising one of her arms in the air, where it remained motionless, until he lowered it again. He noticed her eyes fluttering, and through the brief slits he saw the Orient, shining. So, he had beheaded the Boss of Tu Shin for her, and, he saw this quite clearly, placed the head on a pole in the Boss's garden.

Covered in fans, she saw in a mirror pool, sparkling, the eastern world. Oh yes, elegantly had she performed, serving the warrior. Then, changing, she was gone. The snowcapped mountains melted and she was in the lowland. Sitting in the door of a temple, legs folded, was a yogi, thin as paper, eyes flashing in exaltation. Devastated by his gaze, she surrendered and became him.

"As you will notice, ladies and gentlemen—" The magician lifted the lid, his forehead pounding. So he had loved her there, too, in the incense of Benares the sacred city, in the seventy-nine positions. "—the box is empty."

He worked the lid, with shaking hands. The stage was covered in visions. In the center was a beating heart from which civilizations were streaming. Upon the Mayan cliffs he saw a priest in gold robes lower his knife into a virgin, naked on an altar of stone.

"Ladies and gentlemen, I hope you will notice—" He turned the box upside down. "—no false bottom, no escape hatch."

The temple of the sun crumbled, was covered by the jungle, faded into the earth. The priest vanished, only to emerge again from the beating heart, into the court of the virgin, now a Syrian Queen, and it was she who bestowed upon him the high honor of her favored circle. With great ceremony and the blowing of trumpets was he castrated.

"Now, ladies and gentlemen," he said, wiping the sweat from his brow, "you will observe the teeth of this saw are sharp as a razor." He brushed the air in front of his eyes, fighting through the cobwebs of memory: In the last century, he had left a townhouse in top hat and evening cape, swinging a silver-headed cane. Following the opera, drawn by the moontide, he retired to a brothel to escape the rain, and there in the parlor she sat, laughing darkly, clad in beads. *Let me take you away,* he said, and *no,* she said, removing her beads, *it is impossible.*

"Very well," said the magician, "a piece of magic rarely seen west of Morocco." He picked her up, laid her in the box. Just so, long ago, in the shadow of the Sphinx, had he tucked her away, into the pyramid.

Upward she rose, with brilliant birds, to their paradise, where she reclined on a couch in the heaven of her lover. *It is for the secret of your illusions that I love you,* she said, as they floated through triangles.

She heard the music of the conch horn, bells, and he, on a platform, thousand-eyed, revealed himself to her as he truly was, and he was, in fact, invisible. *No,* she said, *I must have you,* and there, she saw to her relief, he was the swan and she his lake. *These, my true regions,* he whispered, and became the lotus floating, then the toad.

". . . this perilous operation, learned in Cairo . . ." He closed the lid, sat on the box. Glancing backstage through the curtains and cables, he saw his wife, smiling at him from the wings. Yes, he thought, I'm in a bit of a mess. Sweating coldly, he looked down at the box, inside of which his subject lay sleeping.

And who am I? she asked, dissolving into this life, that life, here, there, palaces and so forth, and then, satisfied that she was eternal, she relaxed, recognizing from the heights: She was no one.

He began to saw.

She heard the slow beating of a drum, saw the jungle, wild plumage. Her body covered in gold fur, she beheld him seated across from her, in the door of a mountain cave, licking his great paw, ferocious, her king, winking at her.

"It is not often I perform this feat for fear of arrest," said the magician. "However, since we are at the end of town . . ." The teeth ripped through the box and sawdust flew in the air.

Back, back, she was gone, more was coming. They were clumsy dragons, loving in lost swamps. His long neck, green skin, ponderable his tail, and her strange egg: The night was pterodactyl, sharp-beaked, she was afraid. Somewhere, she thought, I was a girl.

"I will now ask the gentleman in the front row, that is right, you sir, to come up and examine the depth of the incision I have made in this box." The magician leaned confidently on the box, inside of which the saw was deeply inserted.

The camel will take us away, he whispered, and turning, she saw a kneeling sad-eyed beast. Lifting her silken robe, white, embroidered with dragons, she climbed up to the cab atop the camel's back, where sat the magician, smiling, clad in the cloak of the desert. Slowly the beast stood and walked, like the rocking of waves.

"Very well, my good man," said the magician, "if you are satisfied that no chicanery is being offered here, I shall proceed."

Across the night sand they rode, beneath the lonely heavens, he silent, she in prayer, until they came to an oasis, around which a fierce tribe had gathered, and he was their chief. She descended amid the animals and the oil lamps. Attended by his other wives, she was taken into an arabesque tent. A rug was spread, pillows, their dinner, dates, wine. She listened to voices outside their tent talking of battle and it thrilled her.

"Observe: The torso is separated from the legs."

She was his tenth wife, bore him a son, lived a life of precious price in Bagdad, died an old woman, was buried in a jeweled ebony box. Death was dark and impossible, the coffin opened. He stood over it, in a faded tuxedo, beckoning to her. "You're back," he said.

She stepped out, weakly, onto the smoky stage. People were clapping dully. The room was spinning. She fell into his arms. "Never leave me," she whispered.

He bowed, took her by the hand. The stage was bending. Her legs were trembling and she could not feel her feet. Slowly, he led her toward the stairs. Yes, she thought, he's taking me away.

"Goodbye," he said. The spotlight blinded her. She turned away and saw behind him on the stage a piece of scenery—a balcony window above a courtyard. She stared down a pathway in the painted garden, to the sea, and the white sail of a passing ship. "Take me away," she said.

"Impossible," he said, his face pale and drawn.

She turned to the stairs with trepidation, for they were moving, as if alive. "I thought I was a young girl," she said, warily placing her foot on the top step. "I am an ancient woman."

He released her hand, and turning to the audience, bowed once again, then withdrew across the stage into the wings.

Music began. She descended the stairs. Girls with painted faces came out behind her on the stage, covered in balloons. She stepped carefully onto the floor of the cabaret, which appeared to be tilted on its side. Someone was at her elbow, with his arm around her waist. "Well, my dear," asked her elderly escort, "how did you like being sawed in half?"

A stagehand carried the box into the wings. The magician carried it the rest of the way, into the dressing room, where his wife sat, reading a paper. Beside her in a chair, a child was sleeping.

"How tired you look," she said. "Are you all right?"

"Yes, of course," he said, removing his tie.

She helped him off with his cape and jacket and packed his tuxedo and their other belongings in the magic box. They left by the stage door and walked through the alleyway, the magician carrying the box, his wife holding their sleeping child on her shoulder.

A carriage came up the avenue and the magician hailed it. "To the railway station," he said, handing the box up to the driver.

They climbed into the carriage, sank into the leather seats. The magician stared out the window, toward the river lights. His wife, settling the child in her lap, saw the old gentleman and the girl coming out of the cabaret. "The fog seems to be lifting," she said, drawing her shawl around the child.

The driver cracked his whip. The carriage pulled away, into the night.

Turning
Point

"Supper soon," said Mother. "Stay on the porch."

He would stay on the porch. It was a pirate ship sailing on River Street. During the flood, Mister Noto came down the alley in a rowboat, holding a floorlamp. Now the waters were gone, though there was still mud in the cellar and good chairs had been ruined, Father said.

He climbed the stone porch-railing, to the crow's nest. Across River Street, girls in black dresses came down the steps of the school. He would take their jewels and sail away. At the top of the steps was the nun, who had given him a piano lesson. He had no piano and she told him to practice with his fingers on the arm of a chair. He would make her walk the plank.

The boys came down the steps in their black suits, with long pants that whipped in the wind. His pants were short, his knees stuck out, but his shirt had a red anchor on it, and when the flood came again maybe the house would float away. The boys went into the alley, pushing and shoving, and the girls followed them. He made his fingers into a spyglass and watched them going away, wherever they wanted to, into town or up the hill or to the river where the bums lived under the bridge, and he had to stay behind in his short pants for supper and bed.

The alleyway filled up. No one went anywhere. The boys stood around in a circle and the girls were on tiptoe behind them, screaming.

He jumped down from the porch, into the bushes. The branches held him and then bent over. Through the jungle he crawled, keeping low, to the row of iron spears stabbed into the ground, black and cold. He grasped the fence, a prisoner. Through the bars, he watched the crowd in the alley grow larger.

Gripping the spear heads, he raised his foot carefully, rose up and went over, down onto the sidewalk. Who could stop him, not Mother, it was a getaway. He ran across the street quickly, and ducked into the alley.

The alley was filled with holes, went by the old garages, winding down and away. He pushed into the crowd, but they pushed him back. He got down on his knees and crept like a dog between their legs and came out in front.

Two tall boys were moving slowly around in the center of the crowd, with their hands in front of them. Their arms were long and their hands were curled into tight balls. Their coats and ties were off and he saw the wide suspenders that held up their long pants. His suspenders had ducks on them. Someone in the crowd said, "Get 'im, Johnny."

They stepped lightly, circling right past him, and dust rose at their feet. Was it a dance like the sailor's hornpipe Mother had taught him? One boy swung his arm and it landed with a thud on the other boy's head. The boy stumbled backward into Noto's garage doors. The doors banged, the basketball hoop shook above, and the boy kicked out his foot, saying, "Wait'll I get set."

The hair fell in their eyes, and they tossed it back like horses. They hugged each other and turned slowly around and everyone cheered. It was like books and the radio and movies right in the alley. A sleeve ripped and flapped in the air like a pirate shirt. Arms flew again, thud thud on the head. One of the boys sat down in the dust and did not get up. His shirt was spotted red.

"That's all, Johnny," said someone, taking the other boy by the arm. The game was over and the crowd moved away, down the alley and through the yards, except for the boy who sat in front of Noto's garage with his head down.

The streetlight went on. Mother would be looking out the window. He went over to the boy and said, "Will you show me how?" He curled his fingers in a tight ball, but the boy did not look up.

Mother would be out on the porch, looking up and down the street. He left the boy behind and followed the crowd down the alley, toward a vacant lot, where a fire was burning in a barrel. He curled his fingers into the tight ball and swung his arms through the air. He danced across the lot, swinging his arms and making sounds with his mouth, like the thuds he had heard. What a wonderful game and anybody can play it, he thought, anybody.

The lot was dark and filled with junk. Some boys were standing around the burning barrel. The flames lit their faces and he saw Popeye Santini, the big guy, stirring the barrel with a stick. Sparks floated in the air. Mother would be calling *where are you* in the dark. He went over to Popeye and said, pointing back to the alley where the crowd had been, "Did you see?"

"Beat it."

"I could do that," he said, curling his hands into balls.

No one said anything. He said, "Does anybody want to do it?" He raised his arms in the air.

"Get outa here," said Popeye.

A shadow stepped into the firelight. It was Lurkey Davies, who was his size but could stay out late. Lurkey said, "I'll handle it."

The other boys stood around. He raised his hands, ready for the slow-moving and the turning, but something hit him in the face and a bell rang in his head. He looked around, trying to play the game, but couldn't see, and something hit him on the ear. He reached out, grabbing a shirt. "Wait'll I get set," he said, but a head came toward him, knocking him in the chest, and stumbling backward, he fell on the ground.

He saw streetlight and stars and black telephone wires. Lurkey's face came above him, came closer, lit by fire, and a hand hit him like a stone. He rolled away, swimming in the junk, trying to get up, to move quick. The game wasn't slow, it was fast, faster than his own heart. It rose up, red, choking him. He swung at a passing shadow, thud, heard Lurkey say sonofabitch. He swung at the fire-face again and got hit in the nose and the garages turned sideways. He sank in the junk and covered his head, but two hands grabbed him from behind and lifted him off the ground.

Popeye held him in the air. Another boy was holding Lurkey. "Lemme go," said Lurkey, "I'll kill him." Lurkey's eye was puffed like a cupcake. His own eyes burned like fire. He kicked his feet and Popeye set him down. "Get lost," said Popeye, and gave him a shove.

He walked through the lot, away from the burning barrel. The alleyway was dark and empty. Blood was dripping from his nose. He wiped it on his shirt sleeve. His head was going *bong*. He crossed the street and went up the steps into the house.

Father was reading a newspaper in the living room. Mother came in quickly, said, "Where have you—oh my god, he's been in a fight."

Father lowered his newspaper. "Are you all right?"

"Yes."

Mother took him in the kitchen and washed his face. "Did anyone kick you in the testicles?"

"No."

After supper he went into his room. He played with the wooden soldiers, knocking their heads together. When he fell asleep, the tall boys came through the sky, and turning above him in slow rounds, quietly kissed.

Tiger
Bridge

HER WALK was perfect, having been trained in the school of
Han Tan; her eyebrows, green slivered moons, rose above
the magic pools of her eyes, in which both dragon and
kissing fish swam; her name was Wood Flower and she lived
in a narrow cobble lane beside Yellow River, and a poor
fool, the peddler called Rag Fellow, was in love with her.

Rag Fellow was the bumpkin son of a family of illustrious
drunkards, and hauled an old wagon, arguing with old hags
over copper coins for the rags which he peddled. His home
was the wagon, inside of which he slept at night. By day he
pulled it along the streets, gathering and selling his
abominable wares.

During one such day of selling he chanced to drag his unwholesome cart down the street on which Wood Flower lived. She was on the balcony above her father's store, her face half-hidden by a fan, so that only her dark eye-pools were showing.

They were enough for Rag Fellow to drown in. When he caught sight of her, whatever luckless star was his shone brightly. So intense was the beauty he saw above him, so insane his desire, he soared to the heavenly Blue Isles for a moment, thinking himself an ancient king.

As happens with the beguiled heart when first its secret door swings open, he foolishly transcended his rag station, with which he had been happy. Now he was ready for war. The dummy was a general, decorated with courage. He would have crawled onto the porch and seized her immediately, but she suddenly disappeared within the house and wisely he withdrew. Unfortunately, he did not withdraw far enough.

Down the road he went with his rag business, bestowing gifts of cloth on the startled women, and singing, miserably, but with vigor, a song of his own devising which failed on all counts, and yet . . .

He continued along until he came to his evening camp upon the river bank. Pity he did not journey farther up that stream, tracing it out of the district and into the mountains to its source. There, by a waterfall, he might have lived out his ragged life in quiet thought.

No, he must be a prince of love, and so it goes along Yellow River, where men are so often struck dumb by a single glance from almond eyes. The True Man, of course, then takes to wine, to gambling, to opium, to war, preferring any vice or vanquishment to love-sickness, but Rag Fellow was thoroughly possessed.

His case, of course, was hopeless: Wood Flower was prepared from childhood for the palace of our Immortal Emperor, the Purple Cloud. Her father, a prosperous merchant, had seen to that. Thus, the delightful Han Tan Walk was hers, she moved with the silent and delicious grace so prized at the Purple Court. She was accomplished in the lute, played the old songs, and knew the arts of hair and face, rendering still more desirable her own natural beauty, as rare as any Heaven and Earth have produced in this Illustrious Dynasty.

Back up the cobble lane came Rag Fellow, day in and day out, narrowing his business practice until it spanned only the small square in front of the shop of Wood Flower's father. Originally the Rag Fellow made little money, still less did he make by holding to this single spot, and his eyes, already somewhat glazed, took on the look of a stone temple monkey.

He saw her, yes, many times, walking light as the birds of Han Tan, with her eyes cast downward in religious devotion. Despite her religious fervor, occasionally she caught sight of the young rag man and found his adoration not wholly unholy. Thus, one black day, by a tiny turn of her petal lips, she favored the wretch with the smallest of smiles, perceivable only to a maniac of love such as Rag Fellow now was.

Her smile drove him across the skies in the Ecstasy the blessed hermits call the Wind Wheel. Through the whole of space he darted in an instant. A thousand emperors! yes, that was Rag Fellow now, his doom securely arranged by those excellently thorough demons who lead us down the paths of perdition, making them always appear flower-strewn.

Said another way, for it is a poison of many flavors: He had fallen in love with his death. They say such affairs are common along Yellow River, for the Chief of the Demons has his camp in its mist.

Though Rag Fellow was now a thousand times poorer than before, he was exhilarated into rare fantasy, knowing rages and delights in himself such as kings seldom know, for the door of his heart was not only open, it had blown off its hinges and parades of adoration of Wood Flower went in and out.

The poor loon made a vast search of the neighborhoods, gathering together all rags of some remaining loveliness, which he presented to a sewing woman of the quarter, with instructions to make a robe for a woman of such and such a shape—dimensions which he presented in such lingering detail, the sewing woman could only blush in her thimbles.

The gown was well-made, for the woman's hands were skilled, and the rags, though faded, for that reason had the charm of the ancient in them. When finished, the gown seemed like a sacred relic—as if made for an empress of long ago and held under glass through the ages.

With this powerful suit to be played, Rag Fellow returned to his post outside the shop of Wood Flower's father. The horned goblins who manipulate the hours were not behind schedule this afternoon. Surely, Wood Flower came out, lightly as wind bells, tinkling in her earrings past the peddler, driving him wild with joy, producing such an ecstatic tremble in his body, he almost perished before the appointed hour.

Pursuing her with his rag wagon, he rattled along over the stones, a decent way behind her. Perhaps he aroused no suspicion in the eyes of the streetlamps, but every dog, chicken and housewife on the block knew that Rag Fellow was following Wood Flower, the girl promised to the Imperial Court, sworn to the Emperor's bed for that very night.

In her elegant way she walked toward a distant temple in the hills, for apparently she wished to be far away from the world on her last free and girlish day before entering the Way of the Emperor.

No sooner had she settled herself in the garden of the temple, arranging herself with the spring flowers and the new grasses, than she heard the rumble of wheels, like the chariot of a sky-god.

She prepared herself demurely on the wooden seat, beside a little splashing stream, and with downcast eyes seemed to be far off, in remote reverie, when Rag Fellow appeared like an ancient hero, with his rag wagon, at the gate of the temple.

He left the cart behind him, carrying over his arm the rag offering, walking not like a peddler, but a prince, toward the seated Wood Flower. The bumpkin knew no shame, caution was gone, he went straight to her and said with bursting heart and throbbing voice, "Here is a rag for your floor."

Saying so, he laid the antique robe across her knees. In it were sewn three hundred stories of cloth—flowers, birds, insects, trees, all faded, as if seen through a veil of dreams.

Upset at the young man's impertinence in approaching her, Wood Flower turned upon him the eye of the dragon, angry with fire. When it failed to move him, for he was grinning like an idiot, she could only lower her eyes to the marvelous cloth. She was, after all, mortal and a woman, and of course after a proper interval, she lifted her head and turned her face full toward him, slowly, unable to disguise her delight.

The demons were dancing, all was proceeding according to plan. Rag Fellow was shattered as a lunatic by the moon. Plainly in her eyes he saw the kissing fish rise and he caught her, and she squirmed, wriggling as fish will, and slipped out of his hands, leaving behind on his lips and fingers a luminous film and the perfume of the lake.

Naturally, he called to her. Of course, she turned. He might have been satisfied with one kiss, and yes, she might have known that to go on in this way with a rag peddler was unwise, but . . .

"Beneath Tiger Bridge, tonight," she said, and so the Great Wheel turned, carrying them on toward that encounter envisaged by the Demon Chief.

The day wound on interminably for Rag Fellow and this was good, for though the snail-passage of the hours caused him anxiety, it is his last day on earth.

He ate happily in a shop by the water's edge. Every face, every bowl, shown with a pattern of Wood Flowers. She was in all things, and most of all, in his heart. He could see her there, seated demurely in the shattered doorway. Tonight he would lead her completely inside and they would share the Red Mystery by Yellow River where the fish hawk dives, beneath Tiger Bridge.

Soon he was eagerly crawling down the river bank and under the bridge, though he knew she would not be there yet. She would come later, quietly, wearing the robe of rags. Theirs would be a powerful vow, sealed beneath the Bridge, and he would carry her away in the night in his wagon, forcefully if need be, but in time, when they were living in a distant region of the north in some small cottage, she would see the wisdom and necessity for their flight.

Blind Rag Man! Is it not clear to you by now that your dream of paradise is built upon the caprice of a woman, who whispers *tonight at Tiger Bridge* even while she is preparing her heart for the Court of Our Immortal Emperor, the Excellent Purple Cloud of One Hundred Wives?

No, of course not, he does not hear. He is deaf to everything but the river, blind to all portent, such as the sudden falling of rain. Look how it plays upon the water, stirring up the river. What does he care? He is beneath Tiger Bridge and his feet are dry.

Does he wonder how she will come in the pouring rain? No. She will come to him, will float down the street on boards, if necessary. He does not reckon with the changing face of the moon, for he is the sun of love.

So there he waited, watching her face in the rising water, listening to her voice in the beating of the rain upon Tiger Bridge. It grew dark, he sat in darkness beneath the Bridge, but was burning brightly within, and though the water was at his ankles and he was crouched like a corpse against the

Bridge wall, he was comfortable as an emperor on the imperial couch.

The poets of the Court at that time, men who have since traveled on, left behind them the story of the night on which Wood Flower, the merchant's daughter, appeared in the courtyard of the Purple Cloud. It was raining heavily, the spring rains had begun, but her gown was not spoiled. With averted eyes, a footman carried her out of the Emperor's coach, and another held a silk umbrella over her hair, protecting its subtle waves and the precious combs she wore.

Her gown instantly aroused the profound jealousy of the other court ladies, though it was not contrived in the latest court fashion, nor made of precious silk.

No, the Emperor's latest beauty, lovely Wood Flower, wore a robe of cast-off cloth, of bits and pieces of the ancient city, and it was faded like a dream, filled with sad scenes, of old sky terraces, and diving birds.

The Emperor was satisfied, and an excellent party ensued, with songs and wine, a delightful way to spend such an evening, which was dark and terrible, for the spring rains had come, and Yellow River was rising.

Dare we venture out? We must. Out of the dark courtyard and into the swimming streets goes the tale.

The streets are now a river. And as for the Yellow, it is a torrent, for it has been rising all evening and we are now well past midnight. The Emperor has already retired with his new Flower, and been granted a closer glimpse of the plump little birds who sing in the cloth of her gown. Wood Flower perhaps is sighing, though this cannot be known for certain, but that is how the serving maids tell it, that there was much sighing and some laughter from the Royal Chamber.

Oh, Gracious Lady, how you have risen! Have you risen as high as Yellow River, which climbs now about the neck of Rag Fellow, that foolish fellow who clings to the last pillar of Tiger Bridge, who awaits you in the downpour, whose tears perhaps now mingle with the river?

Excellent Rag Fellow, a fish in your pocket, lamentable Rag Fellow, bathed in the spring swelling of Yellow River, do you think you might now release your grip? The water is at your chin, Tiger Bridge is trembling.

So, then, up it came, over his nose, closing his eyes, finally wrenching him free of the pillar of life, releasing him from his wretched assignation and his unhappy rag suit. Down Yellow River he went.

In the Palace of the Purple Cloud there was laughter. Does she stand at the window now and seek the hidden moon? And are there tears? And for whom?

Down Yellow River went Rag Fellow, tossed and whirled in the spring dance, a good fellow, a fine fellow, heart flooded, dead in the waves, faithful to the end and so deceived. His courage is to be admired. His course was eastward toward the sea.

Day has come upon Yellow River. Yes, and the afternoon is bright. How smooth and clear the water is. The old men are fishing from Tiger Bridge.

Stroke
Of
Good
Luck

A TRUE NURSE ROMANCE

"Lift up your nightshirt, lover, it's time for a shave."

Nurse was young and pretty with large swell breasts. I was fourteen and scared with a large swelling appendix.

She opened a safety razor and put in a blade. "Come on, don't be bashful," she said, and yanked up my white hospital gown. I lay petrified, and she placed her fingers on my stomach, stretching the skin upward. "Don't move," she said, and began to shave, without lather, my secondary sexual characteristics.

I have a mole in there, be careful.

The razor moved swiftly through the dense underbrush. "Don't worry," she said, looking up at me with a smile, "I

haven't slipped yet," and laid her free hand on my primary
sexual characteristic, to keep it safe, no doubt, from razor
rash.

After scraping me bald, she put away the razor and took
a thermometer out of her lapel. "Roll over."

I rolled over onto my side and stared out the window of
my semi-private room, high over the city. Suddenly I felt
something hard and cold going up my semi-private.

"Do you want to see a priest before you go into the
operating room?"

"No."

She pulled down my nightshirt. "Don't go anywhere,"
she said. "I'll be back in a few minutes."

She went out the door and I lay looking out the window.
The night before, I'd gotten a terrific pain in my side. The
doctor came to the house, felt my stomach and said, "Get
him to the hospital." Now the pain was gone, my appendix
was working fine, and would be removed in a few minutes.

Nurse came in wheeling a table. She threw up my
nightshirt and drew out the thermometer. "O.K.,
temperature's normal. Get on." I lowered my nightshirt and
climbed onto the table. She wheeled us out the door and
down the hall. I knew of a man who had a sponge sewn into
his stomach. She brought the table to a stop. "Let me see if
they're ready for you," she said and walked off. I followed
the wiggle of hips inside her tight uniform.

A priest turned the corner of the hallway. Nurse stopped
him and he followed her back to my table.

"Here's a priest," she said happily.

"Hello, my boy."

"You'll have to hurry, Father," she said and hustled off down the hall. I did not watch the wiggle of her hips.

The priest put the band of the confessor around his neck. I said in a whisper, "Bless me, Father, for I have sinned."

His head was turned and his eyes were closed. "Yes, my son, go on."

"About a year ago, Father—I found a pile of old photography magazines in the cellar. They're filled with pictures—of naked women."

"Is that all?"

"I go down there quite a bit, Father."

"Say three *Hail Marys* and pray for me. God bless you."

Nurse turned the corner. "Time to go," she said, and taking the head of the table, wheeled me down the hall. I saw a pair of swinging doors ahead, with portholes in them, and we pushed through, into a large operating theater. Four bright lights were blazing on the ceiling and I was wheeled under them. A doctor came toward me in a white mask and cap.

"Count backward from one hundred, please." A gas mask was pressed to my nose.

"One hundred . . . ninety-nine . . ." The four bright lights became the propellers of an airplane burning in white space.

I awoke in a dimly lit room. A nun was sitting at a table near the foot of the bed. "Hail Mary," I said in a whisper, hoping I wasn't dead.

"Go to sleep," said the nun.

In the days that followed I amused myself drawing pictures of women in skimpy bathing suits, particularly my nurse, whom I regularly depicted in a tiny bikini, running to the sea.

"If I wore something like that, I'd be arrested. Roll over."

I spent each day carefully shaping her long legs, her big hips and breasts, but I was too young and shy to remove her panties on paper and reveal the curling mysterious. Occasionally, however, I slipped in nipples peeking through the halter of the bikini.

"Is that all you ever draw?" asked the nun.

I drew a picture of Jesus and hung it over my bed.

"That's beautiful," said Sister. Nonetheless, I was filled with sinful thought, and now that my secondary sexual characteristics were growing in again, I was spending a good deal of time scratching under my nightshirt. Only the fear of tearing open my incision kept me from having to make another serious confession.

Nurse appeared each morning with a pan of water and a washcloth, to scrub briskly my primary, secondary, and semi-private. For such treatment it was worth having had the operation, and when the time came for me to leave the hospital I feigned weakness and was allowed to stay, at considerable expense to my parents, for another week of birdbaths.

At the end of the second week, my father became suspicious.

"Who are you, Lady Astor?"

"I'm too weak to walk."

"I'll drive you home."

My clothes were brought from the closet. Nurse helped me out of bed and dressed me for the last time.

"Here," I said, and handed her my best work, a sketch of her in a nurse's cap and three Band-Aids.

I limped down the hallway to the lobby, where my mother was waiting happily and my father was paying the bill. He came toward us, shaking his head. "Let's get the hell out of here," he said, taking me by the arm, "before he has a relapse."

We rode home. My mother chattered merrily in the car. My father removed a medicine bottle filled with rye from the glove compartment and took a swig, as he did whenever he paid a bill.

Friends visited me at home and we played Monopoly, but cardboard deeds no longer excited me. I moved my metal hat down Boardwalk listlessly, deep in debt and not caring, longing for green plaster corridors and the smell of antiseptic, and most of all, for my semi-private morning bath.

My drawings of women became more dangerous. I chased bare ladies through the bush, shaping their fat white bottoms hungrily. I hung breasts like cantaloupes on them, with huge cherry nipples, and brushed in the curling mysterious. When my parents came into the room, I hid these works and showed them a caricature of Winston Churchill.

When it came time for a visit to the doctor who had removed my appendix, I had high hopes he'd find something wrong and send me back to the hospital for observation and maybe a trim.

I went into the Medical Arts Building. The doctor felt my

incision, removed the fading stitches with a tweezers, and conducted me into his library, where he told me to wait. I sat down on a leather couch and looked out the window to the street below. Voices came through the open door.

"Take a sperm test, Nurse."

"Yes, Doctor."

A young, good-looking nurse came into the library and closed the door behind her. "Hello," she said, and pulled the Venetian blinds shut. The room fell into half-light. I sat on the couch, waiting nervously.

She opened a medicine cabinet on the wall and removed a long cylindrical tube. "This is cocoa butter," she said. "It will make your scar heal faster." A brown finger emerged from the tube, like a large lipstick.

"Open your trousers, please."

I opened them and she brought the stick of cocoa butter to my incision, gently rubbing the soft, sweet-smelling stick into the red smile on my abdomen. When she finished with the cocoa butter, she went to the cabinet again, this time bringing out a white jar. "Pull your shorts down, please."

Holy Christ.

She unscrewed the lid of the white jar. Cautiously, I lowered my jockeys. Despite my dreams of doctoring a nursie, I was shy, and revealed my secondary hairy only. My private primary was still concealed.

"All the way down, please," she said, and reached into the elastic of my jockeys. We pulled them down together. My private primary was now public.

She opened the white jar and dipped her fingers in. They came out covered with white cream. "Tell me if I hurt you," she said, and sitting down beside me on the couch, slipped her hand between my legs.

Slowly she rubbed the cream up my thighs toward my groin, and for an insane moment I thought her fingers brushed over my primary. Then to my astonishment, she began to rub it, lightly yes, but deliberately. She rubbed the white cream all around it, and squeezed it gently.

"Maybe we should take your pants all the way off," she said, and pulled them off my ankles, along with my jockey shorts. I sat up, half-naked and astounded.

"Lie down," she said, "and relax." My thigh was touching hers. Her skirt was tight, her hips soft, my heart was pounding.

I sank back down and she returned her hand between my thighs and laid her fingers on Mickey Finn, as my Irish grandfather used to call his primary sexual characteristic. My stomach leapt wildly; Nurse covered Mickey's head with cream.

A typically modern male, I tried to repress any sign of excitement. After all, what kind of fiend would the doctor and his nurse think I was, if, during the sperm test, just because of a little cream rub on my primary, I got an erection?

Nurse solved my dilemma by taking Mickey Finn directly in her fingers, toying with him in a manner that could not be misinterpreted. She bent him back and forth, slapped him up and down, and rubbed cream from the balls of Mickey's feet to the top of his swelling head.

I was facing the window but I could feel Mickey growing larger in Nurse's fingers. She seemed prepared for this manifestation, for she now began a rhythmic stroking up and down Mickey's person. The blood rose to his head, my soft stones rolled, and Mickey Finn came out of his tomb like the Resurrection, dressed in a white robe, standing straight as a shillelagh.

I lay with arms folded on my chest, in the first realm of forgetfulness. Nurse tickled Mickey's belly with her finger. She pulled him by the collar, massaged his dome, put cream in his eye. She took his rubber suit and pulled it over his head, then let it back down and did this several times. "I'm not hurting you, am I?" she asked.

I looked at her deliriously. I was fourteen years old and God had answered my darkest prayer.

As if building a fire girl-scout fashion, Nurse took Mickey in the palms of both hands and rolled him back and forth like a stick. She was a good scout. Mickey grew hot at the root. I drifted out the window and returned through the ceiling.

Nurse returned to the jar for more cream. I lay, fixed to her hip. With two fingers, then, she embraced Mickey by the throat, in a most sensitive spot. The veins bulged in his neck. With little strokes, she massaged up and down. Mickey pulsed dangerously. Nurse drew her hand away, stopping us on the edge of explosion and Mickey fell backward on my stomach, descending from his dizzy climb.

Is this it? Do they just test it out to see if it's still working, and you crawl home on your hands and knees?

"Would you help me off with my jacket, please?" asked the nurse. I pulled her jacket off obediently, touching the soft shoulders beneath her blouse. "I don't want to get any cream on it," she said, and then, with a smile, dipped her fingers back into the jar.

She fed Mickey Finn some more cream and instantly he grew fat and happy again, dancing in the half-light, a whipped-cream hat cocked over one eye.

Her legs were crossed, the knees bare behind sheer stockings. We were sunk together in the soft leather couch with hips full against each other. The window was burning, four propellers were turning in space, her entire hand was closing around Mickey and I was taking off.

She stopped us on the edge. "You'd better roll up your shirt," she said.

I tucked it quickly up around my neck, and Nurse closed her hand around Mickey again, pumping him up and down, faster and more forceful, her fingers slithering with cream, driving Mickey to maddening heights.

Up came the naked photographic ladies, laughing uncontrollably. Mickey ticked, going nuts, and then, as so often happened to my Irish grandfather's still during prohibition, there came an eruption from the cellar. Mickey's head blew off, and a white jet of homemade brew flew through the air, splashing down on my bare chest.

She pumped Mickey again and again, until the last drop was out, and my childhood was gone. Then she stood, and opening the cabinet, took out a glass slide. She ran it up my chest, scooping off the sperm for the celebrated test, enclosing it efficiently inside another slide. Then she washed Mickey Finn and tenderly dried him.

"You can get dressed now," she said, and handed me the tube of cocoa butter. "Don't forget to rub this in every day," she said with a smile, and left me.

I left the Medical Arts Building, weak in the knees, but wonderfully wiser. In a single afternoon, I had shot past all my friends into a new and exciting world, and the whole deal only cost my father seven hundred dollars.

The
Trap

Out of the whirling snow came a man wrapped so deep in fur he resembled a bear. He moved slowly along, stepping grotesquely, leaving the print of snowshoes behind him.

Pushing against the wind, he marched toward a log cabin set in a grove of frozen hemlock. Smoke rose from the cabin's chimney and its frostbitten windows were bright. He walked to the door, opened it, and plunged into the warm firelight.

"So you made it," said a man in uniform, seated at a rough oak desk.

"Yes sir," said the man in fur, saluting. "Constable Turner reporting."

"I'm Lieutenant Belfast. Make yourself at home, Constable."

Constable Turner removed his coat and hat, revealing the red jacket of the Northwest Mounted Police. Stepping to the stove, he struggled to remove his boots.

The cabin door opened again and a short potbellied man with an armload of wood stepped in. "Cook," said the Lieutenant, "meet Constable Turner."

"Howdy," said Cook, setting down the wood and extending his hand. "You're new to the Mounties?"

"Yes," said Turner.

"You'll like it," said Cook. "Good clean work."

In the following weeks, Constable Turner was worked into the routine of the post. Assigned to counting caribou droppings, he prowled the snow fields each day with his notebook, determining the size of the herd. He slipped through the trees, and dreaming of gunrunners and fur smugglers, took careful measure of the steaming pellet.

At night, the glow from the cabin was the only light on Red Deer Hill. Inside a card game of quiet bids and swearing filled the evenings for Belfast and Cook, while Constable Turner lay on his bunk studying the Criminal Code.

After the other men went to sleep, he continued reading ensnarement procedure by the low lamp, until his eyes crossed with fatigue. He closed the manual, blew out the light, and looking at the dark sloping roof over his bed, counted a pattern of knotholes in the wood. *Were the other men having him on about the droppings?*

109   THE TRAP

Next morning, Constable Turner climbed from a cold bed onto the freezing floor.

"Bright enough day," said Cook, rattling his pans.

"Plenty of sun," said Constable Turner. "Spot a turd ten miles away." He went out of the cabin toward the woodpile in the rear. Crossing the yard, he heard the distant barking of dogs. Looking down Red Deer Hill, he saw a dog team coming out of the fir trees below.

"Mail sled," said Cook, joining him on the hillside.

"Bonjour, messieurs," said the postman, a natty little Frenchman. Carrying his pouch into the cabin, he presented Lieutenant Belfast with the correspondence from the post in Regina. Belfast slowly and carefully went through the month's orders.

"Constable Turner," he said, getting up and walking to the large wall map of the territory.

"Yes sir," said Turner, crossing quickly to his side.

"There's a man in trouble here," said the Lieutenant, pointing to a northwest spot on the map. "You'll leave tomorrow and take him to the hospital in Edmonton."

"Yes sir."

"You might take a look at this." Lieutenant Belfast handed Turner a wrinkled letter, written in a thin unsteady hand:

20 Sep 1909

Deer sir a trapper name John live up snake lake an is craze for some year might send a man afor He kill someone I saw him summer an he think he a moose I am miner W Nettlebrew

Turner spent the day prowling restlessly around his laid-out pack, adding and eliminating, finally settling the great bundle in the corner by his bed. He spent the evening by the oil lamp, studying the trail map, and traced his 120-mile route carefully with red ink.

With the first grey light of dawn, he was outside preparing the dog team. He slipped the lead dog into the harness, then the rest of the dogs in pairs, seven in all, yapping happily.

"Here's your grub," said Cook, handing him a filled knapsack, which Constable Turner tied in with his own large travel pack.

Lieutenant Belfast handed him the long sled whip. "Take care of yourself, Constable."

"Thank you, sir." Turner saluted, cracked the whip, and before he could say *mush!* the eager dogs were on their way. Along Red Deer Hill they ran, and then down; Constable Turner looked quickly back over his shoulder but the cabin was already out of sight.

By the time the sun was noon high, he was beyond the woods he knew, breaking new trail with map and compass, northwest toward Snake Lake. "Mush, mush!" he cried, whipping the air. The snow flew and Constable Turner's dreams fluttered in brilliant crystal designs, converging into the shape of glistening medals, falling on his jacket.

At dusk he searched along the ridge of a hill for a campsite, settling finally by a large rock in the side of the hill, out of the driving wind. The sun had gone and the bitter cold of the north came on, penetrating through the several layers of his uniform, deep into his bones.

He took dry wood from his pack and built a fire against the rock wall. Laying a frying pan on the flame, he thawed

111   THE TRAP

out the dogs' dinner of frozen fish. His own dinner followed—warm beef and scorched potato. He heated snow in his cup, turning it to water and then to tea into which he dunked one of Cook's biscuits.

Dinner ended, the dogs huddled closer to him, chins on paws, ears back, eyes glistening in the firelight. He took a shovel from his pack and dug a hole in the snow. When the hole was large enough for his entire body, he unrolled his sleeping bag into it. Slipping into the bag, he scooped a blanket of snow over himself and lay down. The wind blew over his grave bed. He turned his face into the sleeping bag and the dogs crept closer. The fire collapsed, went to embers, to ashes, and disappeared beneath lightly falling snow.

Four days he mushed over rolling timberland and on the fifth day came to a low-lying basin of scrub pine. A frozen body of water ran through it, winding like a snake. Above the treetops, he saw smoke curling in the sky.

Constable Turner tied the dogs to a tree, and removing his rifle from the pack, went forward along the icy waterway, blending in with the scenery, now a rock, now a tree. The snow was new and made no sound beneath his boots. He followed the snaking lake to its tail. Beyond it, the woods cleared, and in the clearing was a small cabin.

Circling the cabin, he came up behind it, next to a large storage shed. He crawled through the snow toward the shed, coming up quietly against its back wall. The door of the shed was open.

He stepped through the doorway. His leg brushed a taut rope, which suddenly gave way. A blur passed over him. He tried to leap away, but was struck on the head and fell to the ground, as a large wire cage slammed down around him, forcing him to his knees. He tried to lift the cage. It was weighted from above, with heavy sacks.

"Snaffled," said Constable Turner, struggling to cock his rifle.

He aimed the rifle at the doorway of the shed and held steady as he could, bent over as he was with his head toward the ground. *Performing the duties required of me as a member of the Northwest Mounted Police.* He heard the cabin door open and footsteps flopping in the snow toward the shed. *Without fear, favor, or affection of or toward any person.*

The footsteps stopped. The wall of the shed was filled with knotholes, through which the sun streamed. He ran his eyes over the wall.

The footsteps flopped away. Constable Turner lowered his rifle. "I'll have to break this birdcage to bits," he said, and kicked and shouldered the cage, ramming it with all his might, but the wire did not yield.

The afternoon passed slowly and Constable Turner spent it curled in a ball. Darkness fell and he remained in a huddle. The floor of the shed was frozen earth. The walls were hung with animal skins. The wire of the cage was so finely woven he was unable to pass a finger through it. He took pad and pencil from his jacket.

29 Nov 1909

Found trapper. Snaffled in fox pen.
Formulating plan.

The night wrapped him in. His limbs rattled and his teeth chattered uncontrollably. His nose ached as if it had been struck by a hammer.

Sleep came and he fought against it, for sleep was deep cold. Teeth and eyes of animals came out of the dark moonlit walls. Terror surrounded him for a moment and then it passed, and he spent the night dumbly dreaming.

As pale streaks of morning light came across the floor of the shed, Turner was in a crouch, watching the door and the hill, where the grey light was advancing.

He heard the cabin door open. Across the newly-frosted ground came the crunch of boots. "Hello!" shouted Turner, with a voice like cracking ice. "A team of dogs is tied up at the far end of the lake!"

The footsteps crunched away. Later came the barking of the dogs. Their rough voices grew louder until they were in the snow directly outside Turner's shed. Finally, he heard their satisfied chomping on food.

"Hello!" he called. "I am Constable Turner of the Northwest Mounted Police!"

The dogs growled, tearing at their food. Turner banged against the cage with his fist. "I am from the Post on Red Deer Hill, outside Saskatoon!"

An odd, graveled voice came through the wall of the shed:

"Horn soup!"

Then the footsteps crunched through the snow, back to the cabin. Constable Turner sat, staring out the door, his neck bent, and listened to the morning. A rabbit crossed the doorway, looked in for a moment, and hopped away. The sun went along, over the trees, over the shed.

Night came again and the cold moved deeper into him, like icewater in his veins. The snow owl hooted. The trees gleamed in the moonlight. The wind came through the open door, howling around him. His dream was grey and lonely. He ran across the moonlit snow. Yonder were the Caribou Mountains.

An iron sound split the air. Turner sat up, looked around. It was morning. The cage was lifted. His rifle was gone. A shadow stood over him, and a gun barrel gleamed.

"Section 105 of the Criminal Code," said Constable Turner, standing stiffly. "Pointing a firearm at a law enforcement officer."

"Soup's on," said the cracked gravel voice, and the shadow walked out of the shed.

Constable Turner followed numbly through the snow, into the cabin. The cabin held stove, bed, table, chairs. A frying pan sizzled on the stove. The trapper was a small grey-bearded old man with bowed legs, gnarled hands, and a walrus moustache.

"You're under arrest," said Constable Turner.

"Set down," said the trapper, and turning to the stove, emptied the contents of the frying pan into two plates.

Constable Turner ate slowly. The trapper sat across from him, shoveling food into a toothless mouth. In a rocking chair near the stove sat an old hound, fat, sleeping. The rocker moved gently back and forth with the dog's breathing.

"I'm sorry," said Turner, when dinner was ended, "but my orders are to take you into Edmonton."

"I knew a feller went to Edmonton," said the trapper, and getting up, walked to his bed table and opened a cigar box. He handed a faded blue envelope to Turner. It was postmarked Edmonton, 1898.

Turner opened the envelope and removed a single sheet of paper. On it was written, in painfully twisted letters, the words: *Made it OK. Partner Chonkey.*

"Partner Chonkey," said the old man, putting the letter back in the cigar box. "Took our fur to Edmonton five-six year ago. Ain't seen his hide since."

The trapper cleared the table. His shotgun was leaning against a chair. *Get the jump.* Turner weighed the move carefully in his mind. The old man was splashing water in a basin. *No. Can't jump a man while he's doing your dishes.*

The wind howled against the window. The trapper threw the dishwater out the door. Constable Turner stared around the cabin, looking for relics of madness, but there was only a moose head on the wall.

His belly full, fatigue overcame him. Unable to keep his eyes open, he spent the day dozing fitfully in his chair, as the warmth slowly returned to his body. When night came he dragged his chair next to the stove, and extending his feet toward the warmth, tried to formulate a plan. The trapper joined him with his own chair and the two men sat quietly in front of the radiant iron.

"Reckon Partner Chonkey's comin' back?" asked the trapper.

"Maybe," said Constable Turner.

The light in the cabin was low, held in a glass lamp. Constable Turner watched the shadows dance along the log walls. The shadows leapt, died, leapt again.

"He ain't never comin' back," said the trapper, and spit on the stove.

Constable Turner watched the bright fire through the teeth of the stove. The flames were yellow, tinged with blue, and the stove an iron head.

"Chonkey danced with the women, I betcher," said the trapper.

The moon passed through the window, lighting the frosted glass.

"Runnin' through the wood," said the trapper. "Then you're in water. You know what I mean."

"Yes," said Constable Turner, staring at the frozen window.

The dog shifted in his chair and it rocked quietly.

"I kin git those moose to vote," said the trapper. "Trot 'em up to Parlemint, git 'em some wigs."

Wood fell inside the stove, crackling and spitting. "Here come the guests," said the trapper. "Now jist one thing, Consterble," he said, touching Turner's sleeve. "No shootin'. I don't want guests gittin' winged with silver bullets." The trapper opened the door of the stove and called into it. "Come on in, Miss. Please set down."

Constable Turner looked into the glowing firebed. The embers were red and sparks jumped up the stovepipe.

"This here's the Mountie I was tellin' yer 'bout last night," said the trapper to the stove. "Says he's up here for moose. Tryin' to git the vote out, I suppose."

The hound jumped off the rocker and walked across the cabin floor to his food dish. The chair rocked back and forth in the moonlight.

"Ain't cold, air you, Miss?" asked the trapper, speaking toward the rocking chair. "Say, do I hear the Cap'n?"

He turned back to the stove and opened the iron door

once more. "Thought I heerd yer, sir. Step inside. Glad to have yer with us." He nudged Constable Turner. "They're gonna lead me over Caribou Mountain. They been out here a hunnert year, since the territory opened. He come from the sea and she from New Yawk. Pretty, ain't she?"

"Yes," said Constable Turner.

"You betcher," said the trapper. "She reminds me o' the gold rush days. A bag o' gold, gents, will buy the vote of any moose!" He stood and walked to the window. Suddenly his voice fell to a whisper. *"Jesus, here come the wolf!"* He fell back in his chair, as if shot in the chest. "He come to git me! Oh boy, he come to take old John away!"

Turner put his hand on the edge of the trapper's chair. "Don't worry," he said. "I'll take you to a hospital tomorrow."

"Tain't worried," said the trapper. "The lady and gent'll take care o' me. They'll take me, Mountie, where I'm bound to go." He closed his eyes and his head fell forward. "No hospital, Chonkey," he said, softly. "Gubbermint stuff. Party o' seals . . ." His breath came more slowly, grew heavy, and soon he was snoring.

Constable Turner dragged him across the room and laid him in his bunk. Then he banked the fire for the night, and laying his sleeping bag on the floor beside the stove, crawled inside it.

The fire crackled softly. The wind moaned in the chimney. Constable Turner closed his eyes and sleep closed him in its shadow. The shadow became a woman with a pale body of ice and hair like the shining snow field. Beside her walked a sailor with a ring in his ear. They made signs to him, and pointed. He looked where they pointed and was tugged toward the stars, into a great hall, where crystal chandeliers were hung. There upon a rocking chair of ice was the trapper, in long underwear, drinking tea.

Constable Turner came awake in the first grey light and crawled out of his sleeping bag. He opened the stove and stirred the fire, then put the tea kettle back on. A noise came from the old man's bunk.

"Mornin', son," said a muffled voice from within a long brown snout. Large antlers rose up from the pillow. The trapper was wearing the moose head. "Yessir, quite a convention," said the moose-man, climbing out of bed, the long snout coming directly under Turner's nose. "Had every moose for miles lined up there."

The trapper hung the head back on the wall, and they cooked breakfast, ate, and went outside to feed the dogs. The day was clear and bright. Turner and the trapper stood in the snow, while the huskies barked and tore at the meat. "Moose meat," said the trapper.

"I'm mushing over to Edmonton," said Constable Turner.

"Makes yer ears grow," said the trapper.

"I can take your furs," said Constable Turner. "I'll sell them for you and bring back the money and whatever supplies you need."

"Much obliged, Consterble," said the trapper. "If yer can't trust a Mountie, who can?"

They walked to the fur shed behind the cabin. "Watch yer step," said the trapper, pointing to the trip wire. The cage was back up on the ceiling. "Glad yer came by," said the trapper. "I been waitin' years to spring that thing."

They carried the pelts from the shed and loaded them onto the sled. The trapper returned Constable Turner's rifle. "Say, Consterble, git me a new calendar when yer hit town. Mine's wore out."

"I'll see you in two weeks," said Constable Turner, climbing onto the back of the sled. Through the trees he could see the sparkling tail of the Snake.

"If yer run inter Partner Chonkey, tell him to take care o' hisself. Feller drinks like a moose."

Constable Turner cracked the whip, and the weighted team moved off slowly, west from the winding Snake.

It was six days through level country to Edmonton. Constable Turner sold the furs at a good price, had a hot bath in the hotel, and went down that night to the bar. The old piano was tinkling and the saloon girls smiled at his uniform, but he drank alone by the door, beneath a stained-glass lamp, watching the Indians, miners, trappers and trail bums coming in and stumbling out, into the falling snow.

Turner drank slowly, turning the whiskey glass around in his hand. He took pad and pencil from his pocket.

15 Dec 1909

Arrived in Edmonton, without trapper

Turner laid down his pencil. He knew he was through with the Northwest Mounted Police.

The following day he turned in the dog team at Fort Edmonton, along with his uniform, and collected his eighteen dollars pay for the month.

"Where you headed?" asked the Quartermaster.

"Alaska," said Turner.

"Gold, is it?" smiled the Quartermaster.

Turner bought a rifle and a five-year calendar with the head of a moose painted on it. He replaced his provisions, and started on foot through the snow fields, toward Snake Lake.

Two weeks later he came to the glistening Snake's tail, and walked along its frozen shore. Atop the tail, the cabin came into view. The chimney did not signal, however, and when he opened the door, the stove did not greet him with heat.

He took off his pack and cooked dinner. Evening shadows were falling across the lonely clearing. He hung the moose calendar on the wall. The moose head was gone.

He sat for a while in front of the stove, and then stretched out on the trapper's small bed. Exhausted, he fell quickly asleep. He awoke later in the night, when the moon had climbed the window ledge. Its pale ray was deceptive, and for a moment he thought he saw four figures in it—a woman in white, a sailor, an old hound, and a moose on two legs, walking over Caribou Mountain pass.

Soldier
In
The
Blanket

THE MUZZLE of a small machine gun stuck out from behind the floor lamp. A brass cannon fired; a shell floated through the air, knocking the machine gunner on the head. A tank rolled over the rug. "O.K., men, here she comes," said the boy.

The front door bell rang.

It was Annette, the beautiful girl.

"Hi, Jeff." Her perfume floated over the battlefield. The tank banged into her foot, tried to crawl up her ankle. The little man in the turret rose up and aimed a rifle at her, then sank back down.

Mother came into the room. "Hello, Annette."

"Hello, Mrs. Kaye."

"I hope you brought a nightie. We'll be out late."

He collected the soldiers into a box and carried them through the kitchen into the cold spare room where toys were kept.

He played on the painted linoleum, in the Hi Diddle Diddle square. First he became the dark sky. Then he was the white moon, laughing. Finally, the smiling cow.

Annette came in. "Playing Hi Diddle Diddle?"

"No," he said.

"We're going now," said Mother, kissing him on the forehead. Father jingled keys in the doorway.

He watched them through the window, following their red tail lights up the dark street.

"Want to play Uncle Wiggley?" asked Annette.

Around the board he chased her, under the log and into the hole, and at the end he passed her.

"Nuts," she said.

The door bell rang again. Annette went to answer it.

He heard another girl's voice. He climbed on the black horse and rocked along the secret trail. Invisible riders came over the plain of squares. Recognizing them, he waved and called. Through the white room, past the windows, on dancing horses they rode.

"Jeffrey, this is Gloria."

He climbed off the hobby horse and walked away.

"He's shy," said Annette.

On the bench along the wall lay Pinocchio in a heap of wooden limbs and strings. He lifted the long-nosed boy and walked him along the bench. Shadows fell on the wall, like a man and his son. The girls left the room and began talking.

He walked to the Old King Cole square in the center of the linoleum, where he kept his throne. He climbed into it. An airplane passed over in the night. The voices of the girls seemed far away. He felt himself falling through space, with a chute opening behind him.

"O.K., Jeff," said Annette, calling through the doorway. "Time for bed."

He climbed off the throne and went into the bedroom, where his pajamas were laid out. They had a story on them, about a boy and a girl going up a hill to a well.

"Now I lay me down to sleep," he whispered on his knees. A horse-shaped nightlight burned on a table between the twin beds. Moonlight came through the window. Far away, a dog barked. He heard footsteps coming down the alley. A man in a hat walked by the window.

He listened to the footsteps fade away, then blessed himself and crawled into bed.

The front door opened. He heard the girls saying goodbye. He played with his red-hatted soldier under the blanket.

Annette looked into the room. He dropped the soldier and pretended to be sleeping.

She came in quietly. He watched her from under half-closed lids. She switched off the horse-lamp. He could see her in the moonlight.

She unbuttoned her dress and stepped out of it. He saw her underwear. She pulled on a nightgown, like Wendy Darling in Peter Pan.

She passed out of the moonlight, into the darkness by the

beds. She raised the covers and slipped in beside him. His soldier rolled over.

She was a stranger in this bed. Did she know about the various positions? Where her arm lay, he could place riflemen. On her legs he might station his flanks.

"Jeffrey?" she asked in a whisper.

He lay soundless in the blanket, as dreams began to peek up out of the darkness.

"Jeffrey," she whispered. "I'm afraid of the dark."

She pressed against him, down in the valley where his soldier was hiding. His heart was pounding. He wanted to tell her the true significance of Hi Diddle Diddle.

"Play with me, Jeffrey," she whispered, taking his hand and laying it on her body. He walked his fingers like troops over her mountains. *O.K., boys, up this way.*

The
Great
Liar

IN WHATEVER Professor Doctor St. John Noonday said,
there was not even one-hundredth part of the truth. He was
master of the small lie of little consequence; was proficient
in the long convoluted lie in which vast systems of falsehood
spiraled, minutely detailed, leading nowhere. St. John
Noonday lied to men, women, animals, inanimate objects,
and St. John Noonday was not even his name.

For the sake of efficient narrative, it is stated that Doctor
Noonday was born George Moltoch in the coalfields of
northeastern Pennsylvania, though nothing in
Moltoch/Noonday's so-called life can be fastened on with
any degree of certainty. The careful biographer investigates

thoroughly, but the birth story may have a false bottom, beneath which what abyss lies, none but Noonday knows.

However, the inhabitants of Coalhole, Pennsylvania will tell you that a George Moltoch once lived there, and that even as a child he showed signs of genius. He was usually found with the coal miners, those advanced liars noted for extravagant tales of odd creatures seen beneath the earth—ghostly cries, fleeting lights, secret passages and so forth—and little Moltoch went among them and held them spellbound, for he was a born liar.

"He had every liar I ever knew beat a mile," recalls Mr. Ben Shimbers, in his rocking chair on the porch of the Coalhole Old Miner's Home, "and I knew some of the great ones—Bull Kennedy, Black-tongue Dingo, Jimmy the Shovel, we get a lot of them around here—but that boy could cover you in it. I remember a story he told about some cockroaches ten foot long flyin' down the highway in Argentina, a laboratory mutation see what I mean, he had all the little detail, the most natural liar I ever saw. I always looked for his name in local government, but he didn't take it up, just sort of disappeared. Seems like a shame, don't it?"

In high school, Moltoch apprenticed for his First Degree of Mastery in the Dark Art of the Lie, convincing his teachers and classmates that he was going to enter the clergy.

This, of course, was merely a four-year exercise on his part, his first elaborate simulacrum. A model of piety, each morning he read some small quote from the Bible out over the loudspeaker of the school, and gave the blessing at all ball games, for he knew that if a Lie was to be successful, it had to be flawlessly lived, to the hilt. Thus, the caption under his Coalhole High School graduation picture:

George Moltoch—*a classmate hears the Higher Calling.*

Immediately upon leaving high school, Moltoch dropped his clerical mask. He had now mastered the First Degree, could tell a lie without the slightest contraction of will, and to give greater reign to his power of distortion became a salesman for the *Great World Book Encyclopedia.*

He was a dynamic seller, traveling the state, and it was his custom after work to relax in some local gin mill, where he continued to refine his art. Typical was the night in a Carbonville barroom, where Moltoch spun a web of deceit in which he emerged as the Eastern League's leading third baseman in assists, runs-batted-in, and stolen bases. A local authority, who knew the size of every player's bat in the League, past, present, and to come, spoke up, claiming he could not remember Moltoch's name in any boxscores.

The fellow was courting disaster. Moltoch rose to unparalleled heights of distortion, with innumerable statistics and atmospheric phenomena—as he spoke one could hear the turning of the wheels of the old *Phoebe Snow* as it carried his ballclub over the rails for a nightgame with the Scranton Redsox, while from his body there seemed to rise the very essence of the locker room, a vague aroma of linament.

After several years of studying from A to Z the fifty volumes of the *Great World Book Encyclopedia,* Moltoch, with his vast irrelevant erudition, gained the Second Degree of the Lie by permanently metamorphosing into Professor

Doctor St. John Noonday, Cross of Weimar, DBS, former head of the Second Dunterdunstaff Expedition to the Pyramid of Sunten. He began a lecture series, visiting small Pennsylvania towns, addressing such groups as the Moosic Women's Historical Claque.

Wearing a beard and eye-patch, Doctor Noonday spoke to the ladies about the opening of the tomb:

". . . as we wedged our picks into the ancient portcullis, defying the curse, I heard a groan from the camels . . ."

The room in the back of the American Legion Post was quiet as a desert, except for the sound of the bowling alley next door, while around Doctor Noonday's head the lost secrets of the dead seemed to swirl in a mist. On through the evening he spoke, wrapping his audience in great lengths of gauze, until they were totally embalmed.

After the meeting was over, Doctor Noonday took a breath of air in the back lot of the Post, accompanied by the recording secretary of the Claque, Miss Edwina Bender. Noonday's modest car was parked in the lot, and as he bent Miss Bender over the fender, talking softly of the Nile, he unwrapped her mummy, finally wedging his pick in her portcullis. Her groans, so like the hump-loaded camel, were covered by the sound of bowling balls.

Professor Noonday's lecture series won him wide acclaim and a chair of merit in the History Department of Pennsylvania State University. His examination was brief; so powerful was his encyclopedic exposition of ancient civilization, his colleagues never dreamed of questioning him. His transcript, forged, his degrees, clever copies, seemed perfectly in order to the professoriat, and he was welcomed enthusiastically. Especially enjoyed was his dissertation on Gammon Philodon, the Gnostic philosopher who had never lived.

Noonday's books, *Planes of Historical Intersection* and the *Immortal Riddle of Philodon,* as well as a brief monograph on Mayan highways, were out of print at the moment, though new plates were being struck in England. The Chairman of the History Department remarked while tipsy that he had seen a few pages of the original manuscripts and they were "of the first magnitude."

Once established in the easy pace of University life, Noonday was able to devote more time to his personal meditations. These exercises were unspeakably complex, containing exquisite patterns of *suggestio falsi,* removed from truth and removed again. During one such meditation, by superb economy of truth and the ladder of false logic, Noonday proved beyond his own rational doubt that he was not only the opener of the tomb of Sunten, but was, in fact, Sunten himself, dreaming of a twentieth century which had not yet dawned.

A bird tweeted on the window sill; a student demonstration bomb went off in the street below—an ordinary day, yet in one room of University Park, Pa., sat a Pharaoh, laughing with the thunderous laughter that is said to come during the first moments of mastering the Planes of Historical Intersection, the Third Degree of the Lie.

Noonday saw that he was all men, that he had invented the wheel, walked with Plato, performed experimental surgery at Buchenwald. It was an immense delusion and he was perfectly comfortable in it.

Some critics may say Noonday was mad. He was not. Toweringly weird, yes—mad, no. He saw that in five years he would attain the Presidency of the University. From there he could embark on a career leading straight to the White House, that High Seat of the Lie, open only to holders of the Third Degree of Falsehood.

Note: Mastery of the Third Degree of the Lie comes, as it did with Noonday, when the candidate convinces himself he is a Universal Man. Sustained by this imposture, his rise to world power is generally quite rapid. (Though such technical exposition is admittedly of questionable literary taste, your careful biographer includes it for the sake of the serious student.)

Leaving his rooms, Noonday walked to the Campus Diner for some dinner. He ate codfish cakes, left a kingly tip. As he stepped onto the sidewalk outside the diner, his eye fell upon a large member of the roach family, a waterbug scurrying along. The shadowy creature slipped into the cellar of the diner and Noonday stood transfixed by a sudden dark illumination of the Fourth Degree of the Lie:

Insects are fish.

The night seemed made of plastic. Staggering, he held to a tree.

Trees are roast beef.

He was caught, he realized with sudden alarm, in the Immortal Riddle of Philodon, by which the gods are confounded. Feeler and fin had crossed in the night, been united, and Noonday had realized, through the powerful insight of the Fourth Degree, the mutual penetration of all lies.

In a night of revelation, in which he walked till dawn around the lonely campus, he gained the atomic vision of the Adept Liar, seeing in every tree, in every doorway, in every face, the same empty dance of electrons—lovely whirling motion, like the tongue of a good liar from which spin galaxies of humbuggery. Between cockroach and codfish there were only structural differences—their substance was the same and *this substance itself* was a lie.

He saw the entire Universe wheeling, made of a fine shimmering pattern, a Lie of such grand and incredible artistry his own vain dream of political empire collapsed—the White House was a doll house played in by childish fibbers. He left the University that morning, disappearing without forwarding address, becoming a homeless wanderer.

Down the highway he went, headed for New York. He rode in trucks, slept in fields, wandered in the swamps of New Jersey, his spirit moving back and forth from blissful joy to dismal depression.

Note: Students of the Dark Art have always commented on the stormy nature of the Fourth Degree. The Adept has in one moment the certain knowledge he is a Prince of Falsehood, adorned in the cloak of rarest illusion, while in the next he is filled with bitter emptiness. This emptiness, of course, is the unconscious hungering for the Fifth Degree.

On arriving in New York, he joined the ranks of forgotten men. While walking on the Bowery one morning, Noonday felt a sudden surge within himself, and being familiar now with the changing of the bands, he knew a new Degree of the Lie was dawning. Looking around, he was struck by the act of a devastated hobo, who was doing a ruined little dance at a stoplight, threatening to wipe the windshields of halted cars with a grease rag if not given a nickel or a dime.

Noonday watched, transfixed. The light changed. The cars started up. The bum waltzed through the moving traffic, heedless of danger, waving his rag. Then, almost in slow motion he was lifted by the fender of a taxi cab and hurled through the air, landing in a fetal position in the gutter, his leg terribly twisted.

"Are you all right?" asked Doctor Noonday, bending over the derelict.

"Three months in hospital, Johnny," said the old fellow, smiling. "Soup and hot towels."

With the siren of the approaching ambulance in his ears, Noonday walked up the street. He knew the time for the Supreme Test had come. At the stoplight, he stepped off the curb into the stream of yellow cabs and roaring trucks. A large fruit truck was upon him. He made no attempt to avoid it, merely steeled himself into the most powerful Lie of his long and variegated career.

At the moment of impact, instead of being struck and tossed into the air, he passed directly into the cold slow pulse of the truck body. His own body density dropped into the realm of densely packed iron, and suddenly he was the hood ornament, a frozen Mercury with winged helmet, then the whirling fan belt, pumping pistons, sighing cylinders. His humanity was swallowed in the thunder-song of the engine and he thrilled on the fiery altar, incandescent, terrible.

He proceeded along the drive shaft, stopping only for a brief interlude with the cargo of tropical fruit, where he hung for a moment in a sweet dream of the Caribbean; then finally exhausted, he found himself in the street, somewhat dizzy, though perfectly intact, as the fruit truck bounced away down the block.

"You got to use a rag, Johnny!"

Noonday turned back to the curb, where the ambulance

crew was lifting the broken bum onto a stretcher. The bum waved his grease-cloth at Noonday. "A rag helps—careful, John, that leg is hollow—helps you balance . . ." He disappeared into the ambulance, and with wailing siren it rolled away.

Noonday walked along. He had faced the Great Death, as the Fifth Degree of the Lie is called, had offered himself to the powers of destruction only to find they didn't apply, for Death was a Lie.

A dilapidated bum shuffled past Noonday, dragging his wretched body over the sidewalk. Noonday followed slowly behind him, amazed at the bum's endurance. His feet were coming out of his shoes, his pants were ripped from ankle to tincrack, revealing the ugly sores on his legs. And yet, thought Noonday, he lives on, afraid of death. *But death is a Lie!*

Noonday's heart erupted. He swelled out with a strange new feeling, out and out, along the sidewalk until he enveloped the bum like a cloud, until he held in himself the sorrow of the bum's Lie, and then he passed on, along the Bowery, over all the sad sons of bitches of the morning, drinking in their bitter cups, gagging on their stinking gall.

Bums invaded his head, their dizziness was his, their muttering, their hopelessness, their thirst. Suffocating in their pickle brine, he walked the street, wrapped in the Bowery's filthy mantle.

He walked uptown, where he was engulfed by men hustling along with brief cases, pushing hot dog carts, peeping in girlie-book windows, riding in limousiness, drilling in the ground.

You are caught in lies! screamed Noonday at the skyline, his heart turning over, sobbing for the coffee man and his mobile urn.

"Lies!" cried Noonday, waving his fist at the swarming crowd, for it was lunch hour and secretaries and executives were out walking and shopping. No one paid him any attention, of course, just another crackpot on Sixth Avenue, yesterday a man demonstrated against mini-skirts.

Noonday crossed 50th Street, sat down on the edge of the Time and Life Building fountain, and listened. Like frantic ants, people made their way along all around him. He heard the great daily grindstone turning, the cruel wheel of Lies men call position, wearing down the day.

A small spot of pain began in his left temple, and moved slowly across his forehead to the other temple, where it locked a vise grip on his brow. Then from the base of his skull all along his crown came a rolling agony, grinding the cells of his brain.

Holding his head in his hands, Noonday rocked back and forth like a child, on the edge of the fountain, his coattails hanging in the water.

The whole program of Lies was his now. He had tuned in on the mad music of earth, screeching, beeping, scratching lunacy. From around the city and around the globe, Noonday was receiving. He heard the children of the Lie moaning low and he wanted to save them, but he didn't know what to do. His brain exploding with overload, his heart bumping wildly, Noonday jumped in the fountain.

The Sixth Degree of the Lie dawned.

Sweetly as a bird lifting its song in morning, it rose up in him.

"What's going on here?"

"I don't know, Officer, this guy thinks he's a fish."

In the midst of nylons rushing down 50th Street, in the babble of guided tours, in the sound of the policeman's voice, Noonday heard the silence—a thundering silence, and he passed into profound emptiness.

"Come on, Mac, go home and sleep it off."

He was nothing. There was nothing. Behind the lies, giving birth to beautiful thighs and gleaming badges, there was a pure quiet spotless state, and that, thought Noonday, stepping from the fountain, that, laughed Noonday stumbling dripping wet up the avenue, that, that, that!

Elephant's
Graveyard

THE BATTLE ELEPHANTS of King Sudarma of Daspur were
dining in the royal courtyard. The chief elephant,
mistaking a stained window of the palace for a large green
leaf, drove his trunk through the colored glass, lacerating
his long nose. The blood did not trouble him, for he was
used to spears in his hide, but his pride was deeply
wounded, and when his trunk was wrapped in a large white
bandage he was humiliated.

In the days that followed, similar incidents occurred. The
bull elder bumped into the palace walls, shaking the court
ladies in their chamber, and crushed by accident, with his
foot, a royal hay wagon.

"He is losing his sight, my Lord," said the mahout, a hawk-nosed, grey-bearded old man, for fifty years the trainer of King Sudarma's battle elephants.

"Our army has grown old," said the King, as the two men descended from the balcony to the courtyard, where the royal guard had so often assembled with bright flags and gold harness and marched out of the palace gates to battle. But the royal saddle with silver warrior bells no longer tempted King Sudarma, for parades now gave him a backache, and he was content to let his kingdom slumber in peace.

The King and his mahout crossed the sandy courtyard to the side of the wounded bull elder, who stood munching some leftover hay in the sunlight. In the past the younger bulls had waited until he was finished before they ate, but now it was he who was last to dine. Once he had led them all in battle, waving an uprooted tree, with the King on his back in a gold canopy. Now he was tired and the hot day passed slowly.

The King stroked the nose of the wounded bull. "Can the future be read in an elephant's eye?" he asked, brushing a large black fly away from the bull's heavy brow.

"I have led an unholy life, gracious Lord, and know nothing of oracles," said the mahout. He opened the bandage on the bull's trunk and applied a healing paste made by an old woman of the village.

In the second watch of the night, the old bull was struck in the belly by a pain the size of a thousand spears. Mad with anguish, he broke his stable chain and staggered past the other bulls, into the courtyard. His body quivered from trunk to tail. Where was the enemy? He raised his head and fixed his eyes on the stars, for if he did not he would fall and he did not want to fall in the courtyard. The cows were watching from the doorway of the stable. They had all been his wives. He moved himself slowly to the high wooden fence of the pen and rested against it in silence.

The mahout rose from a restless sleep, his chest and stomach cramped with indigestion. No doubt it was the eloquent curry of the King's cook speaking. He turned on his bed of straw, trying to dispel the pain. A dream rose in his mind, haunting him again. Some holy men had been chasing him with prayers and rattling beads; he'd managed to elude them in the garden of a courtesan. He shook his head, glad to find himself in his own room; he was getting too old for courtesans. He swung his feet onto the floor and leaning on a smoothly polished ebony cane, rose and walked through the bamboo door into the courtyard. There was a great shadow against the fence. He picked up a lantern and ran toward it.

The elephant smelled the mahout clearly but could see only a dim shape below. He struggled to hold himself against the creaking pillars of the fence, scraping his tusks along the wood. He wanted to go beyond the fence. He wanted to lie down where he could not be seen by the calves and gossiping cows.

"I must see King Sudarma," said the mahout to the white-robed eunuch who attended the lotus-leaf entrance to the royal bedchambers.

From the outer wall of the palace, a midnight raga droned in the still North Indian air, and in the labyrinth of corridors bells jingled on the feet of the serving girls. The mahout was shown down a lamplit hall, and through a jewel-beaded door to the evening presence of King Sudarma.

The King sat in dark blue evening cloak before a low table, on which the book of sacred knowledge, the Holy Vedas, lay open, marked by a golden thread. The mahout knelt before it, not quite touching his head to the polished floor, for he was not a religious man.

"What is it?" asked the King.

"The eldest bull," said the mahout, raising his head, "will die tonight."

King Sudarma did not look up. The illuminated script danced beneath a flickering brass lamp.

"It is his wish to go outside, my lord," said the mahout.

"Lead him away, then," said the King.

The stable boys had awakened and were holding a water bucket up to the bull. He dipped his trunk into the water, but did not drink, and the bandage grew wet at the edges. The mahout came across the courtyard and gave the order for mounting. A ladder was placed against the elephant's side and the mahout climbed up onto the bull, settling himself on the neck.

The boys swung the high palace gates open. The elephant did not move. The mahout whispered into his ear and struck him lightly with his cane. The elephant lurched forward, and seeing the open gate, marched slowly out of the courtyard into the moonlit plain.

"Come for me at dawn!" called the mahout to the boys running in the dust beside the elephant. Gradually the boys were left behind and the mahout heard the gates of the palace closing. The song of the sitar faded and soon he and the elephant were alone beneath the stars and the full pale moon.

The mahout charted his way in the sky. The elephant walked stiffly in the sand. His feet were heavy. Dark men had loaded him with a stone. He pulled it over the sand and the dark men danced around him. The stone was heavier than a great tree and he strained against its weight.

A white figure appeared to him out of the shadows of the plain. Ahead, winking flirtatiously, was the fattest of the King's royal cows. She shook her haunches. The old bull trumpeted and hurried toward her, waving his bandaged trunk. He tried to mount her, but she vanished.

"What is it?" asked the mahout, scratching the elephant's battle-scarred ears.

The elephant looked into the shadows, but the plain was empty. He moved slowly forward, sniffing the air, but there was no scent of the cow, only the dry sand, and the great stone he dragged along.

"We came this way before, old fellow, do you recall?" said the mahout, remembering with a sigh the reckless ride he'd taken with his ruination, the dancing girl of the palace. Indeed, thought the mahout, it seems last night we passed this way, though it was full twenty years ago the wench coaxed a ride in the King's gold canopy.

The courtyard was dark and quiet. He roused the stable boys. "Here, worthless ones, black hashish for your dreams. Prepare the King's elephant and say nothing."

The royal canopy was fastened to the back of the eldest bull. A

veiled figure climbed the ladder and slipped through the embroidered
curtain of the canopy.

"Open the gates," *said the mahout, climbing up behind her.*

The gates were opened and they rode all night, the elephant
searching for stray grass, his ears twitching to the sighs upon his back
from within the pale curtains.

"Lovers must make certain noises," said the mahout,
scratching the favorite spot behind the elephant's ears.
Indeed, he thought, the palace trembled when you climbed
upon a cow in the garden.

The night was hot. The mahout led the young cow out of her
quarters and chaining her between two trees, brought out the bull elder
and let him loose. Now the lamps were rattling in the stable for the
ground was shaking and it was rumored the ears of the palace
maidens were wrapped with silk bands to prevent them hearing the
moaning in the garden. The mahout crept across the courtyard, certain
they were listening anyway. He stopped by the evening incense bowl,
beneath a lotus-shaped window. The bull and his bride would ride all
night. He watched discreetly from nearby to see they did not knock the
palace walls down in their passion.

"Such sounds are tempting," *whispered a voice from above him.*

He turned and looked up. There was a face behind the curtains.
"We are prisoners of love," *he said, handing a stick of smoking*
incense through the window. She put it in her teeth. He could see
her clearly now. The mark of Shiva, Lord of the Dance, was
on her forehead and her transparent gown was whirling in
the stars. "Ah well," he said, patting the elephant on the
side of the head, "we've both grown older."

The elephant walked slowly. Long ago he and the other
bulls had run like thunder here, the colors of the King

streaming from their trunks. Now he plodded along, for dark men had tied stones to his feet. He lifted his trunk. In the dryness, he smelled fruit.

"No," said the mahout, peering in the dark grove of trees ahead, "don't stop." Holy men lived in such hideouts and holy men made him itch. During the spring festival of saints, holy men flocked to the village and he had to ride off quickly on the King's elephant to escape a scratching fit. Undoubtedly, he was a terrific sinner. Indeed, he loved the dice, a disgrace for a man of his age, but he was unusually clever at throwing them with the palace soldiers.

The elephant's trunk dragged in the sand. He tried to shake the load of stone off, but it stayed with him. He moved his feet forward, but went nowhere.

"Up," said the mahout, urging with his knees, "up the hill."

The elephant moved forward. The mahout watched the moon suddenly grow bigger on the edge of the hill and he felt himself go up and touch it.

"I've found you again," he whispered.

"If you dare." She opened her veil. They climbed toward the moon and touched it.

The elephant raised his head. He saw the round ivory face and dark smiling eyes of a cow on the crest of the hill, and he struggled up the slope.

The mahout rocked on the elephant's neck. The moon leapt away beyond them, and below, shining, was the jungle. The mahout did not fancy the jungle, and signaled the elephant with his cane.

The elephant lifted his trunk, tasting the many smells

that filled the air. The flowers called him with their deep perfume. He marched forward, toward the jungle.

The mahout beat his cane on the elephant's head, but they were already moving down the hillside and he realized it was too late. The ragged shadow of the jungle came closer, and the fallen moon grew larger.

The elephant trotted toward the dark garden, pulling the great stone along. The ivory cow was waiting for him in the trees. Dark men could not hold him. The trees came closer, the leaves touched him. He was inside. She was ahead through the leaves and he suddenly remembered. Untamed. All else . . . men . . . Kings . . . the enemy . . . had been a trick! He plunged into the steaming mist, stamping his feet, crushing the flowers, kicking off the dark men's load. A trick! he raged, calling to her, pushing down the trees.

The mahout clung to the elephant's back, trying to see ahead in the pitch darkness, and saw only the white bandaged trunk waving in the air. He hugged tightly, pressing himself to the coarse, bumping hide. This, he realized, his heart shuddering, is a wild elephant. The tangled leaves and branches ripped his legs; a cool body slithered across his ankle. O mahout, he cried in himself, this is what comes of spending holy days in opium dens with the rope climbers.

The elephant crashed through the bush, tearing at the leaves. *King, King,* cried the parrots from their perches.

I was the King, thundered the elephant. The trees parted. Below flowed a river and he stumbled toward it, plunging into the swirling water with a groan.

"No!" shouted the mahout, yanking on the elephant's

ears. The jungle water rushed up over the mahout's legs, chest, chin, and he went under. The moonlight shattered in the water. He was in the basin. Mother washed him. How pleasant it was. "No!" He lifted his head above the water with a gasp. The swift current tore him loose from the elephant's head. He grabbed the trunk and clung to it, and putting the snout to his lips, kissed it desperately.

The elephant recognized the old man's smell, but the deep stream was cool. He could stay down, without the dark load, in the river, below the mud. The old man had given him a nut. Then the battle drums rolled. He could hear them rolling in the roar of the river. He trembled on the edge of death.

"To the shore!" cried the mahout.

The elephant struggled to lift his feet out of the mud. Chains of weeds dragged behind him and he moved slowly through the water. His eyes rose above the tide and he shuffled through the mud. The heavy darkness was on his shoulders again and the load was hurting. He moved his front feet up onto the shore, but could not raise his back legs out of the mud.

I am alive, thought the mahout as the river fell away. I have escaped. "Up," he said, begging the elephant forward.

The elephant pulled his back feet, but the load would not move. It was too heavy. He looked up and down the river bank. The cows were not watching. The stable door was closed. He sank down.

The mahout fell forward, clinging to the elephant's trunk. The elephant lowered his haunches with a thunderous splash and mud rained down on the mahout from all sides. The river bank made sucking noises and the elephant rolled over on his side, his back legs still in the water.

It was the third watch of the night. The mahout sat on the river bank, keeping the flies away from the elephant's eyes. In the distance the arrogant tiger called. The elephant raised his bandaged trunk in the air, answering with a weak bleat.

"Hush," said the mahout, gently stroking the swaying trunk, "he's far away."

The elephant lay on his side, staring into the mud, waiting for the dark men to unload him. The heavy cargo made him sore, and the dark men swarmed around him, talking their intricate tongue. He was strapped all over. They'd loaded him down in the mud and stabbed him in the belly.

The mahout stared across the river, waiting for the dawn. His head hurt and his chest was aching and he swore no more hot food, for his indigestion was deep and terrible now, cutting up and down in dark waves of pain. He clutched his stomach and rocked back and forth, trying to remember a prayer he'd learned as a child, recalling instead a dice game he'd played with the soldiers.

The elephant tried to keep away the stinging flies with his trunk. Tail and trunk were all he could move. The mud was cool and they were unloading his back legs. He closed his eyes. Soon they'd be done and he could sleep.

The mahout rocked in the mud. I have thoroughly degraded myself. He pressed his elbows into his stomach, trying to piece together the prayer, but her face kept returning, and the sound of the dice.

"My darling," she whispered, turning in the firelight.

"You," he said and collapsed in the mud, clinging to himself. Bringing his feet up under his chin, he stiffened in the river bed.

The elephant raised his trunk. A sweet belch of hay broke the air. He saw a bright light and in it white cows dancing with trunk to tail. He put his bandaged trunk in the ring. His load fell away, and he rose above the dawn.

"I'll bet a hundred!" cried the mahout, as the white cube turned slowly in the air. His indigestion was gone and he'd had good luck. There would be pearls for the dancing girl and wine for the stable boys. The black-dotted eyes flashed, stopped on Kali, the toss of death. Bidding goodnight to the soldiers he walked with a sack of money in his pocket to the village to see the old woman about a potion.

"Come in," she said, smiling in the doorway of her hut. She was crippled and he helped her take the canister down from the cupboard. "Make this tea," she said. "Whoever drinks it will be filled with profound longing for you."

"Indeed," said the mahout, "that is what I need."

He walked through the village toward the palace. This time she would be his completely. Quickly he mounted the steps toward her chamber, pulled open the door. Her mirrors and beads were on the bed, but the room was empty. He went to the window. Below in the courtyard the palace gates were opening and a procession of soldiers and stable boys came through, carrying a litter covered with white linen. That is she, thought the mahout running down the stairs into the courtyard. She loves to ride behind curtains.

The stable boys were weeping. The litter was lowered to

the sand in the middle of the courtyard. A breeze lifted the linen, revealing a brown face and the head of an ebony cane.

"Ah no," cried the mahout. "I have died!"

From the four quarters of space, holy men appeared. "We will take you to the royal chamber," they said, holding out their arms.

"Never!" shouted the mahout, lifted into the air by a terrible wind.

"I will take you," said the elephant, kneeling in space.